"Am I a cha———
Is that your reason?"

Jamie demanded an explanation for Logan's apparent interest. She knew it wasn't love! "Why are you playing games with me? Why *me*?"

"I'm not playing games," Logan answered as he ran his fingers gently down Jamie's cheek. "Kiss me, Jamie...."

The breath caught in her throat. "No," she refused at last, trying to twist free of him.

"Jamie—a kiss, that's all. You have no need to be afraid of me."

Jamie's heart urged her to respond to the ardent demand of this handsome, inscrutable man—in spite of her doubts. Not only was she uncertain what he wanted, she didn't even know for sure who he was. *No reason to be afraid,* she said to herself. *That's what he thinks!*

Master of Uluru

by

HELEN BIANCHIN

Harlequin Books

TORONTO · LONDON · LOS ANGELES · AMSTERDAM
SYDNEY · HAMBURG · PARIS · STOCKHOLM · ATHENS · TOKYO

Original hardcover edition published in 1980
by Mills & Boon Limited

ISBN 0-373-02378-2

Harlequin edition published January 1981

Printed in U.S.A.

CHAPTER ONE

DAMN! Jamie slid out and stood regarding her stricken vehicle with a mixture of rage and very real apprehension. The thought of being stranded in Outback isolation was daunting to say the least.

Moving round to the front of the station wagon, she lifted the hood and systematically began checking plugs and terminals amid the tangle of wires, becoming perplexed when her examination brought nothing to light. Slipping back behind the wheel, she twisted the ignition key again and again trying to get the engine to fire, each attempt proving equally fruitless, and with a muttered curse she slumped back in the seat.

The likelihood of another motorist coming to her aid in the immediate future was negligible. She was carrying plenty of food and water, sufficient for three or four days, so at least she wouldn't starve or go thirsty. At worst she had to face the night and perhaps another day alone in this parched wilderness.

Dear Lord, it was hot! The flies had long ago scented human occupation, and Jamie continued the idle swishing movement with her hand in an effort to keep the majority at bay. The dry enervating heat conjured up thoughts of water—she wasn't fussy, right now she'd settle for immersion in a cattle-trough! A sense of humour is a fine thing, she reminded herself silently, but hysterics are definitely out!

It was an hour or more before a slight sound alerted her attention. Listening carefully, she strained her ears in an effort to determine which direction it was coming from, eager for visual confirmation. Excitedly she slipped out from behind the wheel and prepared to wave at the oncoming vehicle, for soon it must become visible and she didn't want to risk having it speed past.

Several minutes went by and still nothing appeared. A puzzled frown creased Jamie's brow as she delved into the glove compartment for her binoculars, adjusting the lenses before scanning the horizon. Yes, there was a definite cloud of dust to the south, and she could hear the sound of an engine, faint, but definitely an engine.

At that precise moment she caught a flash of yellow, and focussed her attention on it, glimpsing with remarkable clarity a large grader an instant before it became obscured again beneath a cloud of dust. Relief washed over her like a tide. Rescue was at hand, less than a mile away, although the direction in which it was travelling was dubious.

The decision to walk for help occurred instantaneously, and without thinking too deeply about the consequences of leaving her vehicle, Jamie carefully filled a water-bag from the large plastic container in the rear of the station wagon, slid her sunglassess down from their resting place above her forehead, then squashing an old faded denim cap over her hair, she caught up her shoulder-bag and cheerfully set off.

Within five minutes the sweat was trickling down her body beneath her clothing, and she had never felt so hot in her entire life. The sun beat relentlessly down upon her head and shoulders, searing through her thin cotton blouse. Sunburn—she should have thought of that, she grimaced. It didn't help remembering the tube of cream she had tucked away among her belongings in the station wagon.

If one wanted to pause for reflection and study the surroundings, there was a stark beauty in the red-brown soil, the dry dusty spinifex that grew in clumped profusion. The Outback—barren, and vaguely cruel. An unchanging terrain that encompassed thousands of miles, it had a magic all its own. One either loved or hated it, there were no half measures.

The noise of the powerful engine filled Jamie's ears, and she glanced ahead to view the huge ugly earth-moving machine with a sense of frustration. Surely the driver could see her? But who out here would think to check their rear-vision mirror more than once or twice during the entire day?

A light laugh bubbled in her throat. No doubt she'd have to walk right up to that ugly monster, skirt it, and probably stand in front of it before the man operating the controls would see her and bring it to a halt. And then he could be forgiven if he thought his eyesight was playing tricks on him!

The sudden stillness came as a surprise, nonetheless.

'What the hell——!' a deep-timbred voice bit out angrily. 'Where in the name of God did you spring from?'

Never had Jamie been more aware of her diminutive stature. The grim-faced stranger standing less than three feet distant towered head and shoulders above her, his build matching his height. There was lithe strength evident in the powerful frame, and no amount of dust and sweat could disguise a potent magnetism that was devastatingly male.

'My vehicle broke down about a mile back,' she began. 'I——'

'And you *walked*?' The force of his voice exploded around her.

Jamie started to explain, only to have her words waved aside.

'Of all the crazy females!' His derision was plainly evident as eyes of the most vivid blue she had ever seen speared her mercilessly. 'Have you no conception of the dangers involved in abandoning a vehicle out here?'

What an ill-mannered bear of a man—albeit a ruggedly good-looking one!

'I'm neither crazy nor foolhardy,' she began defensively. 'With the help of binoculars I could see your machine from my station wagon.' With false sweetness she queried, 'Would you have preferred me to telephone first?'

Regarding her steadily, he lifted a hand and pushed his broad-brimmed hat further back on his head. 'You answer back, too.'

'Only when provoked,' she conceded evenly.

'Well, Miss——?' An eyebrow arched enquiringly, and she hurriedly supplied her name.

'Prentiss—Jamie Prentiss.'

'Jamie?' he mocked, and she tilted her head to one side.

'Perhaps you chose your own name?'

He raked her slender curves with something akin to frustrated resignation. 'Well, Jamie Prentiss,' he uttered wryly, 'what do you suggest I do with you?'

Her eyes widened behind the large lenses. 'My station wagon——'

'Yes.' He gave a sigh of exasperation. 'You do realise how isolated we are out here, I suppose? I hope you don't think I can conjure up a garage mechanic, effect repairs, and wave you on your way?'

His sarcasm wasn't subtle, and she was all too aware he regarded her as a nuisance. 'Look,' she began evenly, 'I didn't deliberately wish misfortune upon my head. I would have much preferred to drive right past you. Believe me,' she assured him fervently, 'if I'd thought the engine would pass out on me, I'd never have hired the wretched vehicle in the first place.'

His eyes began a slow appraisal of her physical attributes, noting the slim curves, the glowing skin and the expressive elf-like face beneath the brim of her denim cap.

Jamie squirmed inwardly, conscious that she must look far from attractive in her hot and dusty state with her long hair pushed on top of her head. However, she forced herself to meet his gaze squarely.

'Travelling alone out here isn't exactly the epitome of wisdom,' he drawled. 'With several conducted tours available, why didn't you book and come out to the Rock with the next busload of tourists?'

'One—I work for a living. Two—my friends drove on ahead of me,' she elaborated. 'And three —I don't particularly like conducted tours. I much prefer to gather as much information as I can and explore without the regimentation of a timetable.'

His laugh was husky and faintly sardonic. 'I should have guessed—you're a Kiwi,' he allowed, and his amused cynicism rankled.

'I'm a New Zealander, yes,' she answered stiffly.

'Climb up into the cab, Jamie Prentiss,' he commanded wryly. 'Standing out here in this blistering heat exchanging pleasantries won't get your vehicle fixed.'

She couldn't resist the barb, 'And me out of your hair?'

'That, too.'

Well, he was nothing if not brutally honest. She

watched as he swung his large frame effortlessly into
the cab of the huge machine, and she accepted his
helping hand unhesitantly. An ungraceful ascent by
being stubbornly independent would gain precisely
nothing!

'This cab wasn't made for two,' Jamie managed
lightly in an attempt to hide her sudden confusion,
for at such close quarters she was made tinglingly
aware of him. Obviously he didn't intend to indulge
in idle conversation, for all she received by way of
acknowledgment was a piercing glance. 'Where are
you going?'

'To base camp—I'll use the Land Rover to get
back to your vehicle. I presume there's a toolkit in
the trunk?' He raised a querying eyebrow, then
grimaced. 'Never mind, I'll take along one of my
own.'

'I'm sorry to put you to any inconvenience,' Jamie
found herself apologising, and felt vaguely cross
with herself for doing so. What did he think, for
heaven's sake—that she'd engineered a breakdown
just for the fun of it? He was brusque to the point of
rudeness, and she couldn't fathom why. Perhaps he
was just having a bad day, or maybe he disliked
women ... Whatever it was, he could scarcely be de-
scribed as friendly.

'You *are* an inconvenience,' he maintained bluntly. 'Merely by being female. With luck there won't
be much mechanically wrong and you can get on
your way.'

Jamie seethed in silence for several seconds, then
she ventured sweetly, 'Do you have a name?'

'Logan.'

'Just—Logan?'

The smile he threw in her direction held bored
cynicism. 'Question and answer time?'

She met his gaze and held it. 'I've travelled several thousand miles around this vast continent,' she offered matter-of-factly, 'and met all kinds of people from all walks of life. Up until now, I haven't been able to fault Australian hospitality.' She glanced out over the parched ground. 'Please believe me, Logan whoever-you-are—I can think of several places I'd rather be than in the middle of nowhere with a boorish brute for company!'

'My, my,' Logan accorded reluctantly. 'You certainly pack a punch for such a scrap of barely-discernible femininity!' He inclined his head, then doffed a dusty hat. 'Please accept my humble apologies. I can only plead temporary ill-manners due to the heat and the need for a thirst-quenching can of beer.'

Jamie spared him a scathing glance. 'Sincerity isn't one of your virtues, is it?'

'Let's cut the idle chitchat,' he countered brusquely. 'We're ten minutes from camp, and the noise this thing makes precludes conversation—unless you have a preference for shouting.'

With that, he leaned forward and switched on the powerful engine, engaged the gears and sent it lumbering into motion.

'Sit down!' a voice bellowed close to her ear. 'It's bad enough having a female on my hands—but heaven protect me from an injured one!'

Whatever initially made her think he was attractive? she pondered wonderingly. The man was an unfeeling, caustic brute, straight out of the wilds. The thought brought a faint smile to her lips.

They reached camp eventually, although each minute seemed like twenty, and Jamie's ears felt ready to burst with the noise of the monsterish machine as Logan switched off the ignition.

'Do you need a hand?'

She looked into the face several inches below her

own, and declined. She'd rather jump down than accept his help. Once down on the ground she gazed with interest at the assorted trailers irregularly grouped together, their colour almost obscured by a coating of fine red-brown dust. There was a large truck, a Land Rover, and two large vans parked to one side. Some distance beyond them was a small corrugated-iron structure, its purpose clearly obvious by virtue of its separate location. Imprinted on the sandy soil were the tire-marks of several heavy machines, and it intrigued her that such a large outfit was necessary to effect road maintenance.

'If you've finished your inspection, perhaps you wouldn't mind getting into the passenger seat?' Logan slanted tersely. 'I haven't the whole afternoon to waste.'

Rather guiltily Jamie crossed to where he was standing and slid into the seat beside him, conscious that he'd already switched on the engine.

The Land Rover ate up the distance with ease, and she suspected he deliberately accelerated to annoy her, coming to a halt beside the dusty station wagon with a shriek of brakes and a cloud of fine red dust.

'Do you plan to sit there and watch?' Logan mocked as he slid out from behind the wheel. Within seconds he lifted the hood and began a cursory inspection of the engine.

Jamie slowly crossed to his side. 'What would you have me do?' she countered calmly. 'Dance around it and chant some incantation that would zap it into mechanical perfection?' She lifted an expressive eyebrow. 'Sorry to disappoint you, but I clean forgot my witch's gear. Without it, no spell is guaranteed.'

'You have a sassy tongue,' he observed.

'On a scale of eight to one, yours wouldn't even score!'

A flash of humour chased across his rugged features, causing her to blink and wonder if she'd imagined it. Possibly the man was human, after all!

'Get in behind the wheel, Jamie. The gearshift is in neutral, I presume?'

'The temptation to leave it in first is almost more than I can control,' she bit out. 'What are you doing?' she asked incredulously a few minutes later as he emerged from the rear of the Land Rover.

'Tying on a tow-rope,' Logan explained with scant patience. 'Your engine has shot its mountings, causing it to slip forward into the radiator. Nothing short of a miracle will resurrect it.' His glance seared her briefly. 'I need you around like I need a sore thumb. However, male chivalry is not yet dead. I'll contact the office at Alice Springs by radio and get them to telephone the rental firm with details. I'll also arrange for your friends at Ayers Rock to be notified of your predicament. With regard to *you*—I've no option but to tow you back to camp, where you'll have to stay until arrangements can be made to have you transported out either tomorrow or the following day. Meantime,' he added cynically, 'you're free to enjoy the limited facilities our base camp provides. With the compaction unit effecting major repairs, there are around fourteen red-blooded males who'll welcome your distracting presence with whoops of joy and open arms. Just do me a favour and keep a low profile, will you?'

'I'll melt into the background, I promise,' Jamie said slowly.

Logan swept a glance over her slim-curved five-foot-two-inch frame, and there was nothing remotely resembling humour in his forceful features. 'That's doubtful.' He bent down and tested the tow-rope, then straightened to stand regarding her. 'Let's get this thing on the road. All you have to do is steer, right?'

Jamie simply nodded her head—anything verbal seemed superfluous. She watched as he strode ahead and swung his powerful frame into the Land Rover, then the engine roared and she quickly checked that the brake had been released. She had no desire to prove further what a nuisance she was—she'd already been left in no doubt as to that!

The cloud of dust kicked up by the Land Rover billowed up in front of her, making visibility obscure and almost totally nil. All she had to do was steer—how impossible when she couldn't even see where she was going!

It seemed an age before a single horn blast signalled the Land Rover's intention to stop, and Jamie gently applied the brake and brought the station wagon to a halt.

'Well, this is it,' Logan's voice drawled, and she twisted round, squinting through the open window at the brilliant solar orb directly above him.

'If you can bring yourself to release your grip on that steering wheel and get out, I'll show you the ablution van where you can wash—before six o'clock, unless you want to share it with fourteen other men,' he mocked callously. 'You can freshen up while I raise Alice Springs on the radio. But first, give me details regarding your vehicle and the names of the people you want informed at Ayers Rock.'

Jamie slid out rather shakily and followed his broad back towards the dusty trailer that was only one of several of varying age and description. She stood by as he unlocked the door, then followed him inside and waited until he'd written down the information he required.

'I'll remind you that water out here is a precious commodity,' Logan intimated brusquely some minutes later as he unlocked the ablution van. 'Use only what you need, and use it sparingly.' With that, he turned and walked away, and Jamie hurriedly moved towards the station wagon where she delved into her bag and extracted clean clothes and necessary toiletries.

Ten minutes later she entered Logan's trailer feeling considerably refreshed. She had exchanged shorts and blouse for a printed cotton sun-frock with a shirred bodice and thin shoestring straps across each shoulder. Her newly washed hair hung down past her shoulders, and already was beginning to dry, its deep sable brown showing hint of lighter sun-bleached strands that gleamed in the sun.

His scrutiny was swift and analytical, then he gave a mirthless laugh. 'If only you were a schoolgirl, I could treat you with avuncular respect and ensure that my fellow workmates did likewise for the next few days.'

Disbelief clouded her expressive features. 'Days?'

'By midday tomorrow the office in Alice Springs will have informed the car rental firm and received an answer as to what they intend doing—either despatching a replacement vehicle, or arranging transport to the Rock. Your friends will have received a message of your whereabouts, and will have had an opportunity to radio their acknowledgment and perhaps offer to drive through and collect you themselves.' He raked an impatient hand through his hair, light brown and sun-streaked, rumpling it into further disorder. 'Either way, you're here to stay for tonight and tomorrow night—like it or not.'

'I don't,' she replied honestly. 'But I haven't much choice, have I?'

'None at all,' he conceded wryly. He straightened, dwarfing the trailer's compact interior. 'Make yourself at home—such as it is.' He swept an arm negligently, then crammed his hat on to his head. 'There'll be an assortment of machinery pulling into the compound around six—I'll be here to effect introductions.' His smile was totally lacking in humour. 'Meanwhile, don't get any ideas into that pretty little head about hitching a ride with a passing motorist—the price might be more than you're willing to pay.'

A delicate pink tinged her cheeks as anger welled up inside her. Of all the hateful, brutish men she'd ever met, this one took first prize!

'The van furthest south is a kitchen-mess,' Logan enlightened curtly. 'Our supplies will run to feed an extra mouth, and we eat around six-thirty.'

'I have my own food,' Jamie informed him stiffly, and saw him shrug.

'Pass some of it over if you have to be stubbornly independent—although I can't promise it will be accepted.' He moved round her and stepped down on to the ground outside, offering nothing by way of goodbye as he strode towards the grader.

As soon as it had roared out of sight Jamie sank down on to a nearby couch by a screened window. She didn't know whether to laugh or cry at her predicament, and her hands clenched against her thighs as she reflected on her rescuer's manner. To stay here for two days without encountering frequent verbal clashes with Logan seemed an impossibility.

Her eyes wandered around the trailer, noting two bunks at the far end, a small gas stove and a compact refrigerator. The four windows and the door were screened against insect invasion, and although basically clean it needed a feminine hand to banish visible signs of dust and restore the clutter of masculine occupation to general tidiness.

A glance at her watch revealed that it was later than she thought, for it was almost three in the afternoon. The tip of her tongue moistened her lips. She felt thirsty—dare she investigate the contents of the refrigerator and select a cooling drink? Iced water would do, but fruit juice or lemonade would taste like ambrosia.

Logan had invited her to make herself at home, and the temptation was too great. She had several cans of fruit juice in the box of provisions in the station wagon; she could bring them in and exchange them for the chilled cans in the refrigerator. Come to think of it, she could rinse through a few items of clothing that she'd worn the previous day. In this heat they would dry in an hour, and it would give her something to do. Her hands itched to clean up the caravan, but doubtless Logan would regard such a whim as sacrilege.

CHAPTER TWO

AT the roar of heavy earth-moving machinery drawing close to the camp Jamie leapt to her feet and
crossed to a window to view the men's arrival.

One by one the machines came steadily into view
until a total of two graders, two rollers, a bull-dozer,
a loader, two scrapers and four tip-trucks stood
grouped together at the edge of the compound.

After such a high volume of noise the silence was
uncanny for a few seconds, then there was the sound
of men's voices and she moved back out of sight.
Although it was still hot the intense heat of the day
had left the air, and Jamie watched as the men dispersed towards the assortment of trailers.

Her eyes flew to the tallest figure of them all.
Deep in conversation with a man ten to fifteen years
his senior, Logan presented an arresting figure.
Even as she watched, they turned and made their
way slowly towards her, and Jamie pushed back a
few stray tendrils of hair from her face and ner-
vously fingered the straps on her sun-frock.

Logan entered the trailer ahead of the older man,
and he filled it with his bulk, his eyes narrowing
fractionally as he glimpsed her faintly defensive expression.

'Jamie Prentiss—Blake Curtis,' he introduced
formally, offering by way of explanation, 'Blake is in
charge of operations out here.'

The older man's eyes twinkled humorously across
the space between them, and Jamie warmed to him
immediately.

'Stroke of bad luck, Miss Prentiss, getting

stranded out here. Logan tells me your vehicle needs major repairs.'

'Yes, I believe so,' she agreed with a smile. 'I'm sorry if my presence here causes any inconvenience.'

'Not at all,' Blake Curtis dismissed instantly. 'You'll brighten things up considerably—all the boys will fall over themselves to get spruced up.' He gave a husky laugh as he directed a wicked wink in her direction. 'We don't make much of a habit to shave out here. Most of us are sporting a few weeks' growth of beard, Miss Prentiss.'

'Jamie,' she insisted, and he grinned.

'Well, I'd best join the queue at the ablution van. See you later.'

As soon as he was out of earshot, Jamie turned towards Logan. 'He's nice,' she said.

'A whole lot nicer than me, I gather?'

'One hundred per cent,' she responded swiftly, and he laughed.

'Join me in a can of beer?' he queried mockingly. 'After which I, too, will wander over to the ablution van, and honour your presence at the dinner table with a fresh change of clothes.'

'You're deliberately trying to be impossible, aren't you?' she accused. 'I can assure you I don't like having to stay, any more than you want me here. It's obvious you don't like women, and I'm sorry, but I can't help being female.' She drew a deep breath, then let it out slowly. 'Clearly we're going to see a lot of each other over the next day or so, and it would help if we could at least try to be civil.'

He released the tab on a can of beer and offered it to her, and when she refused he lifted it to his lips and drained it in one long thirsty swallow. Piercing blue eyes pinned her glaze relentlessly. 'What makes you think I'm a woman-hater?'

Jamie swallowed the sudden lump in her throat. She had the distinct impression she was treading on very thin ground. 'Perhaps I should re-phrase that particular statement,' she offered cautiously.

'By all means do that.'

'Your attitude leads me to believe you're anti-women at the moment.' She was unprepared for the muffled burst of laughter that escaped his lips, and she was surprised by the gleam of genuine amusement in his blue eyes.

'My attitude? Do all men swoon at your feet, Jamie Prentiss?'

'No. You're twisting my words.'

He leaned out and extracted another can from the refrigerator, released the tab and took a generous swallow, then turned to regard her thoughtfully.

'What are you wearing beneath that thing?'

'It's hot,' she defended, becoming pink beneath his gaze.

'Change it for something that covers you adequately. A skirt and blouse will do fine.'

Of all the bossy, dominating men! She was temporarily speechless. 'Perhaps you'd prefer me to wear a snowsuit?' she demanded.

'You'll be mixing with a group of men who haven't seen a woman in weeks—several weeks, Jamie. Imagine what a sweet feminine thing like you will do to them—especially attired in a skimpy sun-frock that quite obviously states there's not a thing between it and your skin.'

She glared at him resolutely for several seconds, then capitulated with resignation at the cold implacability of his gaze. 'Where will I change?'

'Here—where else?' Logan mocked quietly. 'I'll be a gentleman and turn my back.'

Jamie shook her head. 'No—I'll change while

you're at the ablution van.'

'Shame on you! Don't you trust me to keep my word?' he taunted. He drained the contents of the can, then delved into a cupboard and extracted a clean set of clothes, picked up a towel, then with a mocking salute he flung open the screen door and stepped out from the caravan.

By the time he returned some ten minutes later she had changed into a flared skirt and a simple button-through blouse, and had piled her hair up into a knot on top of her head. The overall effect made her look like a schoolgirl playing at being grown up, and the temptation to poke out her tongue in defiance was almost too much to resist.

Faded blue levis hugged his slim hips, and the dark short-sleeved shirt was unbuttoned almost to the waist, accentuating his muscular frame and adding to the aura of powerful masculinity he emanated.

'That's an improvement,' he approved brusquely as he tossed a damp towel down on to the lower bunk, then he swivelled to regard her with an intent inscrutability that was disconcerting to say the least. 'Food,' he inclined briefly. 'Steak and salad suit you?'

'Have whatever you choose,' Jamie indicated. 'I'll get mine——'

'You'll eat here—with me,' Logan declared, sparing her a cursory glance. 'Steak.'

'What if I'm a vegetarian?' she sallied, and saw one eyebrow raise cynically.

'Are you?'

'No,' she responded evenly. 'But you've made it clear I'm a nuisance. I've no intention of compounding that by eating your food.'

'Polite refusal, or stubborn pigheadedness?' he mocked, and she cast him a level look.

'Both,' she announced succinctly.

'What if I insist?'

'I've no intention of imposing on you any more than is absolutely necessary,' Jamie said steadily, refusing to be intimidated.

'Then be independent,' he dismissed dryly. 'However, I must insist you eat here.' He swung round and moved past her towards the refrigerator, and Jamie slipped quickly outside to the station wagon.

Her carton of provisions held an assortment of tinned food and she hastily selected a can of baked beans, extracted a few slices of bread, caught up a plate and some cutlery, then made her way back to Logan's caravan.

The small gas stove was alight, a large succulent-looking steak already sizzling in the pan. Jamie ignored the way her taste-buds quivered at the appetising aroma, and stoically set about utilising a can-opener.

'There's a saucepan in the cupboard,' Logan indicated without turning his head.

'Thank you.'

Jamie carefully skirted round his powerful frame, drew out a saucepan of suitable size, then retraced her steps.

In silence she watched as he turned the steak, then reaching up he took down a plate and set about opening a selection of tins—beetroot, asparagus, potato salad, and tomatoes. By the time he'd arranged their contents on his plate, the steak was ready.

'The stove is all yours.'

Jamie merely inclined her head in silent acquiescence, and as the beans began to heat she assured herself she preferred her meal to his—and nurtured the secret hope that his meat was as tough as the soles beneath his shoes!

It wasn't, if the way his knife sliced through so easily was any indication—and that it was cooked medium rare, just the way she liked it with the juice running out, seemed to add insult to injury!

Determination ensured that she devoured every last bean on her plate, even going so far as to remove the last vestige of sauce with a piece of bread, and her eyes shifted warily across the table as Logan stood to his feet and crossed to the set of cupboards where he took down a tin of peaches and opened it.

Selecting two dishes, he divided the contents, then returned and placed them on to the table.

'No, thank you,' Jamie declined politely, pushing the plate away.

'Do you want to eat it—or wear it?' His voice was silk-smooth and dangerous, and the glance he shot her was like a bolt of cobalt lightning—menacing and deadly.

'You wouldn't dare!'

'Try me.'

She struggled in silence, sheer perversity causing her to delay capitulating until the last second. 'You're impossible!'

'Then we're even,' he accorded calmly, eyeing her with penetrating intentness. 'There's tinned cream in the cupboard.'

'Is that going to be forced on to me as well?'

'It's entirely up to you.'

'Thanks for giving me the choice!' Jamie picked up the spoon and dipped it into the sliced fruit, and when she had finished, Logan enquired,

'Coffee?'

'Actually, I'd prefer tea,' she decided contrarily, despite the fact that she rarely drank it.

Logan unfolded his length from the narrow couch opposite and filled a billycan with water from a large plastic container, then re-lit the stove.

It didn't take long to boil, and by then Jamie had stacked their plates and cutlery into the small sink. 'I presume the rest of that water is meant for the dishes?'

'It is. Do you want to wash or dry?'

'You mean I can choose?' Jamie queried with deliberate sarcasm. 'That's generous of you.'

'Prickly little thing, aren't you? Are you usually so—waspish?'

'I don't imagine *any* sting would penetrate *your* tough hide,' she avowed.

'Careful,' Logan warned softly, his eyes glinting dangerously, and Jamie clenched her teeth together in a concentrated effort to rein in her resentment of this savagely cynical man.

In silence she sudsed the water, scrubbing the plates until they were squeaky-clean, then she scoured the frying pan with unwarranted vigour. The chore completed, she let out the water, wiped down the small bench, and if she could have hit the silent solid masculine frame standing less than a foot away she would cheerfully have done so. Only wariness over a positive repercussion stayed her hand. He'd hit back, with no holds barred—of that she was certain.

'We'll take our coffee outside,' Logan intimated, and she couldn't resist the barb,

'I have tea, remember?'

'Pick an argument, by all means,' he cautioned hardily. 'Just be certain you can finish it.'

'Sugar?' she queried, endeavouring to keep the unsteadiness out of her voice. What on earth was the matter with her? She couldn't remember feeling so hostile—her nerve-ends taut, stretched almost to breaking point. It was as if this man brought out all her latent anger, and she was at a loss to understand why.

'Two spoons, no milk,' Logan instructed, and when she had added some to her own he picked up his mug, shooting her an inscrutable glance. 'Okay —let's go.'

Jamie didn't bother to query their exact intended location—it was sufficient to get away from the confined space inside the caravan.

However, it soon became apparent from the group of men gathered round a small camp fire, and she was conscious of their curiosity as she entered their circle. Logan brusquely effected introductions, and there was a few seconds' silence before Blake Curtis moved forward.

'Sit down and join us, Jamie,' the head foreman indicated, his smile kindly, and she did as she was bid, endeavouring not to appear surprised as Logan sank down beside her.

A surreptitious glance revealed the men to be a mixed group, their ages varying from mid-twenties to late fifties, and it soon became apparent they accepted the harsh conditions, the heat and the isolation for the financial remuneration. The conversation they offered was animated, and a great deal of interest was shown once it was known that she was on a working holiday.

'How long have you been in Alice Springs?'

Jamie looked across at Blake Curtis and offered a friendly smile. 'We arrived a few weeks before Christmas.'

'You're travelling with a friend?'

She inclined her head. 'Yes. Susan and I have known each other since schooldays.'

'You didn't have any trouble finding work?'

'We had to take whatever was available,' she answered, sweeping her gaze towards the man who had asked the question. 'Although we were fortunate in being able to work together.' She wrinkled her nose expressively and laughed. 'Never having worked behind a hotel bar before, we took a while to get used to pulling beer from the tap—the first day was a disaster!' she recounted. 'An inch of beer in the glass, and the rest froth. Filling one glass was difficult enough, but trying to hold two or three glasses in one hand seemed an impossibility— fortunately most of the men bore with us.'

'You've undertaken a variety of jobs, I suppose?'

'We managed to get secretarial work in Sydney,' she elaborated, ticking them off on her fingers. 'Waitressing at Surfer's Paradise, cleaning in a hospital in Brisbane, serving in a department store in Townsville.'

'And after Alice Springs, where next?'

'Adelaide,' Jamie answered without hesitation. 'Then Melbourne. We'd like to get across to Perth, but if we're forced to meet any major repair bills or change our vehicle for a later, more reliable model, then we probably won't reach there until next year.'

'You've no plans to go up the top to Darwin?'

'We did consider it,' she said with a tinge of regret. 'But our timing was wrong, and we were advised against travelling any further north than Tennant Creek as the Wet season was about to begin.'

'Yes,' another voice agreed, 'it can get pretty hairy during the Wet. I've been bogged down more than once up there.'

Jamie enjoyed their laughter and the easy friendship the men extended her, although she couldn't help noticing that Logan sat for the most part silent, his expression unfathomable.

'Well, I guess it's time to turn in,' Blake Curtis decided at last, getting to his feet.

One by one the men moved away, and Jamie

quickly followed suit. It had been a long day, eventful and somewhat unexpected, and she was more than ready for bed.

The station wagon was parked on the southern fringe of the compound, and within minutes Jamie had unrolled her sleeping-bag and inflated the airmattress, then she climbed into the rear of the station wagon.

It was much too hot to consider sleeping in anything other than the minimum of clothing, and she carefully removed her skirt, then undid the buttons on her blouse before slipping it off. Even reduced to bra and pants she had difficulty ignoring the heat. In an hour or two the temperature would drop, for even in the height of summer the desert air cooled dramatically at night.

Eventually she slipped into a light doze and was on the verge of sleep when a slight sound caught her attention, alerting her defensive instincts, and she gave a mental curse that she had been foolish enough not to lock all the station wagon doors.

Quickly she extended a hand towards the rear door in an attempt to rectify the omission. Her fingers located the button, pressing it down with shaky gratitude, and mindless of her state of undress she lunged for the button securing the lock on the driver's side, muttering beneath her breath as the sleeping bag hampered her movements.

A shape loomed in the dim moonlight on the passenger side and her breath caught in her throat. In an instant the door was pulled open and seconds later she was fighting—clawing and scratching as her intruder forced his way into the rear of the vehicle.

'Lie still!' a coarse voice directed, and Jamie heard his breath rasp unevenly as his hands encountered her bare skin.

'What sort of animal are you?' she gasped, her voice full of loathing as she threshed violently to evade his grasp.

'What's the harm, for God's sake? If you want money, I've got plenty. Name your price.'

Revulsion at the liquor-laden breath nearly made her ill. 'If you don't let me go this second——'

'What will you do, baby?' he sneered, his groping hands seeking the soft fullness beneath her bra.

Incensed, Jamie yelled, uttering a scream that threatened to do damage to her throat as she caught hold of his hair and pulled as hard as she could, simultaneously shifting her body so that she could bring up her knee sharply against a vulnerable part of his anatomy.

'You bitch!' With an agonised groan he rolled to one side.

Jamie's breath was coming in ragged gasps, her stomach heaving as she reached for the door.

The next instant it was wrenched out of her hand and she was half dragged, half lifted out of the the station wagon.

'What in the name of God——' a voice she vaguely registered as belonging to Logan exploded savagely above her head, then she was thrust roughly on to her feet as lights blazed, illuminating the entire compound as several caravan doors sprang open.

'Jamie, are you all right?' Blake Curtis demanded anxiously as he reached them, and she nodded numbly.

'For God's sake, get some clothes on!' Logan bit out, viciously angry as he raked her semi-nudity. Then he turned back and reached inside the station wagon, and Jamie was dimly aware of him hauling out her attacker.

What followed after that remained an indescribable blur. She was conscious of voices raised in anger, and then someone was helping her into a shirt that was several sizes too large.

'Blake, get her the hell out of here!' Logan commanded brutally, subjecting her to a brief searing glance.

Jamie's legs felt as if they wouldn't support her, and she stumbled more than once as she was led towards Logan's caravan. His soothing voice passed right over the top of her head as reaction set in and she began to realise just how close she had come to being sexually assaulted.

'Sit down, Jamie.'

Shakily she obeyed, sinking on to the narrow couch at one side of the table.

'Are you all right, my dear?' Blake queried, and she nodded soundlessly. 'I'll get you a drink.'

Jamie shook her head vigorously. 'I think I'd bring it straight up again,' she managed ruefully, then started involuntarily as Logan stepped into the caravan, dwarfing the confined space with his large frame.

For a matter of seconds he simply stood there, his gaze ruthlessly intent, then he tossed an overnight bag she recognised as her own down on to the lower bunk, and a muscle tightened along his tautly-chiselled jaw as he moved towards the table.

'Okay, Blake, I'll see to her,' Logan charged decisively, and Jamie glanced up with alarm as the head foreman stood to his feet and took his leave.

Immediately the door closed behind him Logan subjected her to a raking scrutiny that brought a tinge of colour to her cheeks.

'I'm still in one piece,' she said defensively.

'By the skin of your teeth,' he grated harshly, resting one hand on his hip. 'Why the hell didn't you lock all the doors?'

She blinked, then ran shaky fingers through her

hair. 'I didn't think——'

'In the name of God, why not?' Logan exploded. 'I warned you to keep a low profile, yet for the best part of an hour you come on like coloured lights on a Christmas tree! There wasn't one red-blooded male out there who didn't fancy his chances with you,' he vouchsafed bluntly, and she gasped out loud.

'You think I deliberately left the doors unlocked to invite——' Her eyes dilated in angry indignation. 'Are you mad?'

'Are you so damned naïve?'

'Oh—go to hell!' she flung shakily, her nerves in shreds. 'I'm going to bed.' She stood up, and was pushed down on to the couch again.

'You're staying right here.'

'With you?' she blazed. 'You *are* mad!'

His smile wasn't pleasant. 'You stay here, Jamie,' he snapped dangerously. 'In this caravan, where I can keep an eye on you.'

'Oh, that's just great,' she decided. 'I've jumped right out of the proverbial frying pan straight into the fire.'

'I'm in no mood for sarcasm,' Logan advised ominously. 'I suggest you change out of that shirt and get some sleep.'

'I'm not staying here!'

'The hell you're not. If necessary, I'll use force to ensure that you do.' He turned and crossed to where her overnight bag lay, and in one quick thrusting movement he upended it, spilling the contents on to the bunk. Collecting a blouse, he advanced towards her. 'Now, will you change that shirt, or will I?'

'You're a brute!' she flung hatefully. 'An unfeeling, callous *devil*!' She snatched the blouse from his hand, tore off the shirt, then thrust each arm into the blouse and did up the buttons.

'What did you expect—sympathy?' he mocked cynically.

'From you—never!' She drew a deep breath, then let it out shakily as she made to move past him. 'Excuse me, I'd like to shower.'

'I'll accompany you.' His gaze was startlingly direct, unwavering, and she was the first to glance away.

'My guide and protector?' she queried bitterly, sorting through her clothes for a skirt or a pair of jeans to cover her bare legs.

He shrugged briefly, and she selected a towel, her bag of toiletries and a change of underclothes. She felt bruised—handled, and there was no way she could possibly sleep without scrubbing her skin with soap and water.

Ten minutes later she re-entered the caravan attired in jeans and blouse with Logan a mere few steps behind her, and she stood uncertainly in the centre of the compact van.

'Which bunk do you want me to occupy?' she queried stoically, not even bothering to look at him.

'The upper,' he declared evenly. 'I doubt it would support my weight.'

'In that case, I'll shift my gear,' she murmured, and proceeded to do so, placing the overnight bag at the end of the upper bunk. Then she fingered the length of her hair, dividing it with the ease of long practice and plaiting it.

'Get up on top, Jamie,' Logan directed hardily as she paused hesitantly.

Without a word she swung herself up on to the upper bunk, and lay down, then caught back a startled cry as a folded blanket was tossed on to her legs.

'It'll get cooler—you may need it,' Logan offered by way of explanation.

Jamie sat up to unfold it, and bumped her head against the low ceiling, bringing a rush of painful tears that spilled over and trickled slowly down her cheeks. It was the final straw.

'For the love of heaven!' Logan cursed with considerable restraint. 'You're a total disaster area. There's no other female I know who could break down in the desert, come within an inch of being raped, then attempt brain damage all in the space of twelve hours!' He moved close, lifting a hand to her head as he probed the slight bump rising on her scalp.

'Ouch!' she muttered resentfully, twisting her head away. 'Leave me alone—I'm all right.'

'Sure you are,' he said disparagingly, spreading the blanket over her limbs. 'Now, lie back and try to get some sleep.'

Jamie thought it extremely doubtful, and she consciously lowered her lids as he switched off the light. The rustle of clothing reached her ears, followed by the faint creaking of boards as he settled down on to his bunk.

For a long time Jamie stared up at the ceiling, aware of the strange curling feeling in the pit of her stomach that Logan's presence evoked. She hated him, she assured herself fiercely, puzzled by the contrariness of her emotions, then gradually tiredness overtook her and she slipped into a deep dreamless sleep.

CHAPTER THREE

'Rise and shine!' a masculine voice instructed from close by—too close, for when Jamie blinked open her eyes, the first thing she glimpsed was Logan's face a few bare inches from her own.

'I've made coffee,' he enlightened brusquely. 'Come on down and have it.'

How could he look so—alert, so refreshed, at such an early hour? She groaned inwardly and inched her body carefully towards the edge of the bunk, then slid her legs over and slipped down to stand on the floor. She felt stiff and tired, but it wouldn't do to let him see that, so she summoned a bright smile and held out her hand for the mug of coffee.

'You look about fifteen,' he declared, his narrowed gaze roving slowly over her slim curves. 'For the record, just how old are you?'

'Twenty-two,' she answered defensively. 'I have a birth certificate among my belongings in Alice Springs to prove it.'

'I'd never have believed it,' he mocked cynically. 'How long have you been in Alice Springs?'

'I'm sure someone asked me that last night,' she frowned pensively. 'From memory, I gave you all a thorough résumé from the time of my arrival in Australia. What are you trying to do—check up on me?'

'No—just interested. I was in Alice Springs myself four weeks ago. I didn't see you around town.'

Jamie met his gaze levelly. 'It's possible I was off duty. Susan and I make the most of our free time.

35

If you can pinpoint the day and the hour, I'll do my best to recall where I was at the time.'

'Sarcasm doesn't become you,' Logan taunted, and she lifted her chin fractionally.

'My apologies—that's your prerogative, isn't it?'

The sound of an engine roaring to life was quickly followed by another, and within minutes the air was heavy with the noise of machinery.

'Time to go,' Logan stated with calm imperturbability. 'Fix yourself breakfast from whatever you fancy in the refrigerator. I'll be back around eleven-thirty. There's a transistor and cassette-recorder with some tapes, a variety of books and a few magazines,' he indicated towards the small table by the couch. 'One word of warning—don't develop an urge to explore beyond the compound. I've no particular desire to set up a search party should you go missing.'

'I do possess a modicum of intelligence,' Jamie sallied, and saw an eyebrow arch quizzically.

'Forgive me,' said Logan in a droll voice. 'Yesterday you abandoned your vehicle and walked almost a mile in the burning sun, thus showing a high disregard for one of the cardinal rules when travelling in isolated territory. How can I be sure that today you won't attempt some form of solitary pursuit equally lacking in wisdom?'

'You couldn't possibly be married,' Jamie proclaimed soberly, refusing to be nettled so early in the day. 'You're too self-assured and sarcastic—no woman in her right mind would put up with you!'

His smile was hatefully sardonic. 'By the way,' he began bluntly, 'you have no need to fear any further advances from your would-be attacker. The man was dismissed on the spot, and left late last night for Alice Springs.' Offering a mocking salute, he turned and disappeared out into the early morning sunlight.

Jamie sipped her coffee pensively. If only it were this time tomorrow, then she would have seen the last of Logan. He made her feel uncomfortable, irritated her beyond measure, and if she never set eyes on him again it couldn't be more to her liking.

She moved idly over to the table and sat down on the couch. It was much too early to consider cooking anything for breakfast, and she felt half inclined to slip back on to the bunk and seek a further hour's sleep. Instead she finished her coffee and then made for the ablution van where she washed and changed into fresh underwear, rinsed the clothes she'd worn the previous evening, hung them out to dry, then she made her way back to Logan's caravan.

For an hour she tidied up inside, swept the floor and removed traces of the fine red dust that clung to everything, then she investigated the refrigerator and made herself a poached egg on toast for breakfast and another cup of coffee.

With the transistor for company, she leafed through the magazines, and glanced idly at the few books Logan had extracted. His taste in reading material tended towards the strictly technical, or spine-chilling adventure novels—for neither of which she could summon much enthusiasm.

At ten o'clock she drew out a pad and pen from her bag and wrote a long newsy letter to her parents, then began another letter to a friend she had worked with for several months in Sydney. These completed, she addressed envelopes, then put the letters into her bag ready for posting when she arrived back in Alice Springs.

It was hot—a dry, almost unbearable heat that made her long for a cool drink and a change of clothes. Correction, she amended silently—a discarding of clothes. She had a bikini in her bag which she would dearly love to slip into, but she could imagine Logan's comments if he arrived back and found her so skimpily clad.

Well, she could at least get a cold drink—the refrigerator was well stocked with cans of every description, and she helped herself to some orange juice.

Then she heard it—the first faint sounds of the machines returning. Soon the air was filled with the noise of heavy machinery, and with an unconscious gesture she lifted a hand and smoothed her hair, tucking a few stray strands beneath the knot on top of her head. She suddenly felt nervous, although why she couldn't fathom. Certainly it couldn't be because of Logan. She disliked him intensely and found him thoroughly objectionable. So why is your stomach behaving as if there's a host of butterflies frantically beating their wings inside? she reiterated silently.

He was almost last among the drivers to bring his machine to a halt on the fringe of the compound, and Jamie tried to tell herself that she wasn't watching him with anything more than a casual interest as he alighted from the cab and moved easily towards the ablution van. She would have liked to have gone outside and given the men a friendly greeting, but instinct prevented her from doing so. Logan's words about maintaining a low profile echoed tauntingly inside her head, and although the desire to disobey him was strong she could see the wisdom in his warning after last night.

The sight of him striding towards the caravan with an easy athletic tread sent her moving hastily to the couch, and she picked up a magazine and was idly leafing through its contents when the screen door swung open.

'You don't appear to have wilted away from the heat,' Logan drawled enigmatically as he stepped inside, and without pausing for a reply he reached into the refrigerator and withdrew a can of beer. 'Care for one? Or there's a fruit juice if you'd prefer it.'

'I've already had a drink, thanks,' Jamie returned politely. 'I had some cans among my own provisions.'

One eyebrow rose slightly. 'While I might not exactly welcome your presence with open arms, I'm not averse to extending hospitality.'

'I wouldn't think of depleting your supplies.'

'I doubt you could do that—you're pint-size, with the appetite of a sparrow.' His glance swept over her, slow and analytical, bringing a blush to her cheeks. 'Personally, I think you could do with more meat on your bones.'

'Obviously your taste in women runs to the generously-endowed Amazon type—blondes, perhaps? They're said to have more fun.'

His eyes gleamed with cynical amusement. 'With the help of chemicals, any woman can become a blonde,' he alluded mockingly. 'It's what lies beneath the artifice that's important—not the wrapping.'

Jamie widened her eyes guilelessly. 'Goodness, does this mean there's more to you than muscle?'

'You're a mite too cheeky for your own good,' Logan drawled. He drained the contents of the beer-can, then placed it on the bench. 'How do you fare faced with steak and a frying pan? Reckon you could manage to toss a passable salad as well?'

'I'm not helpless,' she responded evenly. 'I gather you want me to prepare lunch?'

'It would help. I'm due to contact the office at Alice Springs by radio at midday. They'll have information regarding your vehicle, and a message from your friends at Ayers Rock,' he elaborated. 'I'll show you how to operate the gas-stove. Everything is in the refrigerator.'

Faint anxiety was evident in Jamie's expressive features. 'What do you think will happen about the station wagon?'

'I imagine they'll send someone out and have it towed back to Alice Springs. However, I'll know more after I've come off the radio. Now—the stove.'

Jamie had the small table set and the food ready when Logan returned almost twenty minutes later, and it took considerable restraint not to demand what had transpired.

'Hmm, so you're not just a pretty face,' he observed as he cast a cursory glance over the table. 'Imaginative, too.'

Presumably he meant the dessert she had concocted, the crushed biscuit base filled with a mixture of tinned fruit topped with whipped tinned cream.

'Tell me, Jamie, do you sew a fine seam as well?'

She ignored his faint sarcasm. 'What's the news, Logan? When do I get to leave here?'

'Your friends will arrive tomorrow evening, camp overnight, then head off early Saturday morning. As to your hired vehicle, it will be collected within the next few days and towed back to Alice Springs.'

'So you have something like another forty-odd hours to put up with me,' she shrugged lightly. 'Poor Logan—tomorrow night there'll be yet another woman in the compound. Do you intend reading Susan the riot act, too?'

Eyes of cobalt blue pierced hers. 'I'll leave it for

you to pass on the message. Shall we eat?'

The men drove the machines from the compound two hours later, after observing a siesta-type break during the intense midday heat, and Jamie was once again left to her own devices for several hours.

She found she quite liked the solitude, and took her camera outside in the late afternoon and used several shots—as a reminder, she told herself, something to look back on in years to come. She read for a while, then shortly after five she gathered up a change of clothes and made her way to the ablution van.

At six o'clock when the men returned she stood waiting beside the caravan. Darn Logan and his instructions to remain inside!

The look she received from Logan when she crossed towards the men wasn't encouraging, and she felt like poking out her tongue at him in defiance. He didn't own her, and he had no right to act so proprietorially.

However, it took only as long for him to dismount from the cab of his machine before her arm was taken in a painful grip and she was led—*marched*, towards his caravan.

'You're hurting me!' she hissed furiously, but he didn't release her or bother to speak until they were inside and the screen door had shut behind them.

'Maintaining a low profile doesn't mean you stage a welcoming committee for the men,' Logan evinced hardily, and Jamie rubbed her arm to ease the painful bruising.

'I've been alone with no one to talk to for most of the day,' she uttered peevishly. 'You can't expect to keep me a virtual prisoner, surely?'

'My heart bleeds. Now, stay here while I wash up.'

'Yes, sir—shall I curtsey, too?'

'Cool it,' he advised sardonically. 'I realise you're longing for company, but I'll be back soon. You can fill me in with details of your afternoon.'

Jamie became incensed with an unreasonable anger. 'Go to hell, Logan!'

His grin was the very limit. 'It's the heat—it does strange things to people. That, and being cooped up alone for too long.' With that he stepped down from the caravan, and Jamie heard him whistling softly as he walked away.

There weren't sufficient adjectives to describe how she regarded him, and she felt her body shake with rage. By the time he returned she didn't trust herself to speak, let alone be civil.

She watched silently as he withdrew two cans of beer from the refrigerator and broke open the tabs.

'Here,' he offered quietly, extending a can towards her. 'It's cold, and it'll soothe some of that nervous tension.'

'I don't want——'

'Drink it, Jamie. Even for an unseasoned drinker, there's insufficient alcohol to warrant concern over impaired faculties. Besides, you've got me to watch out for you.'

'Self-appointed guardian angel—although "angel" is scarcely the right word, is it?'

His faint smile surprised her. 'A dark angel, perhaps?' he mused. 'Tell me, how would you feel about an evening at a station homestead? The nearest is twenty miles away, but the owner is a friend of mine, and visitors are always welcome.'

'Are you serious?'

'Of course. If we leave directly after dinner, we can be there by eight.'

'I'd like that,' she admitted, and felt remorse

over her earlier outburst. His reason for taking her along could stem from kindness, or diversely, an unwillingness to leave her behind.

'Drink your beer,' Logan directed. 'In another ten minutes it will be time to go across to the kitchen-mess for dinner.'

The men were bright and cheerful, and there was much laughter throughout the meal. When it was divulged that Jamie was accompanying Logan to the nearby homestead, there was a certain amount of speculation evident in many of the men's eyes, and she longed to discount their conjecture regarding her possible relationship with the giant of a man who was never far from her side. But she remained silent, knowing that as far as they were concerned, actions doubtless spoke louder than words.

Shortly after seven o'clock Jamie slid into the front seat of the Land Rover, and almost immediately Logan set the sturdy vehicle in motion, sending it speeding forward with a deft swing of the wheel.

They headed north over the road she had travelled the previous day, but after traversing several miles he veered off to the right, taking the track that would lead to the homestead.

'What's your friend's name?' Jamie asked idly as she glanced out over the barren ground. How could anyone possibly farm this land? The rainfall was negligible, and she had heard that sometimes several years went by without so much as a drop of water falling to slake the desert's thirst. Stock losses were heavy, and she had seen photographs in magazines and books depicting the harrowing consequences of the drought.

'Blair Frazer. He inherited the property from his father two years ago. You should get along fine with his wife, Jill,' Logan intimated wryly. 'She's a few years older than you, but you'll have much in common.'

She looked at him, considering his words. 'Why, Logan,' she began mischievously, 'is Jill a mite too cheeky for her own good?'

He glanced across at her, and there was little humour in his expression. 'One day you'll come across a man who'll react to your sassy tongue either by paddling your petitely-shaped rear, or kissing you breathless.'

A peculiar warmth invaded her thighs, spreading upwards until it gnawed at her stomach like a raging fire. It made her frighteningly aware of him and the effect he could have on her. In almost slow motion she let her eyes slide over his broadly-chiselled features, noting the strong set of his jaw, the widely spaced cheekbones, down to the mouth with its strangely sensuous yet sensitive lips. Imagining how he might kiss set her stomach turning abrupt somersaults and in no way assisted her overall composure.

'Do they have any children?' she asked.

His sidelong glance held amusement. 'Four—the youngest is around five, and the eldest must be in his early teens.'

'How do they get on for schooling?'

'Lessons by correspondence and over the radio,' he told her. 'When they reach high school level they'll be sent to college, and on to university.'

'Way out here, they must find it lonely,' she ventured, deep in thought. 'No other children to play with, no cinemas or shops, or playgrounds.'

'The city can be pretty lonely, too. Here, the ties of family are very close—there's total involvement.'

An intuitive spark prompted her to ask, 'Was yours a lonely childhood, Logan?'

'No more than most,' he drawled enigmatically. That he didn't intend to elaborate was obvious, and Jamie lapsed into pensive reflection.

Her own childhood had been unusually happy, although at times a lonely one, as she was an only child. Her parents maintained a loving amicable relationship that had been the mainstay of her existence, and there were times when she felt incredibly homesick. Regular weekly correspondence was occasionally implemented by a trans-Tasman telephone call. She missed them terribly, but they understood her need to establish her independence and satisfy the lust to travel. Soon she would go back, even if it was only for a while before setting off on another working holiday. Canada appealed—all that snow and incredible scenery.

'We're almost there,' Logan's voice interposed quietly, and Jamie glanced around her with interest.

The homestead was visible on a slight rise, large and rambling, its deep red brick merging with the redness of the surrounding earth so that the two appeared as one in the dimming sunset. Only the iron roof, the windowpanes, the broad encircling verandah added dimension and identified its structure.

Night came suddenly in the Outback, the clear azure sky deepening to indigo in a short space of time so that there was little illusion of dusk, that shadowy half-light. And the temperature dropped equally quickly, cooling the burning land and lending the air a clean sweetness.

The barking of several dogs heralded their presence before the Land Rover entered the home yard, and by the time Logan brought the vehicle to a halt two people had appeared on the verandah, for visitors were few and far between.

'Logan—I don't believe it!' a feminine voice.

cried out in genuine disbelief, while a deep male voice echoed those same sentiments.

'When did you arrive in these parts?'

Logan slid out from behind the wheel with an easy graceful movement for so large a man, and crossed to grasp the outstretched hand. 'Just over a month ago. I came out with the compaction unit. We're working the section south of here.'

'Well, by all that's mighty—come on in. This calls for a drink.'

'I've brought some company—a stray waif whose vehicle broke down, and who's forced to spend a few days at camp until she's collected by friends visiting the Rock. Jamie Prentiss—Jill and Blair Frazer,' Logan indicated easily, and Jamie stifled a feeling of resentment over the introduction. 'She's a Kiwi on working holiday—currently employed at Alice Springs,' Logan added with a mocking smile that took little of the sting out of his words.

'I've been taken beneath his wing,' Jamie smiled warmly. 'Although I'm unsure whether it's because I'll affect the men, or vice versa. Either way, I feel like a puppy on a leash.'

'She snaps my heels,' Logan drawled laconically. 'Any day now, I'll take her to task.'

'Sounds ominous,' Jill Frazer laughed with open delight as she tucked a hand through his. 'Come inside. We'll sit on the verandah, drink something long and cool, and catch up with all the news.'

It was evident within a short space of time that the two men were friends of long standing, for they shared a companionship that bore the ease of familiarity, and Jamie found Jill to be delightful. The children were home on holiday, and they crowded out on to the verandah to sit with the adults, peppering the conversation with a bevy of questions so that it was impossible for a lull to develop.

Inevitably it became time to leave, and it was well after midnight when Logan drew the Land Rover to a halt in the compound alongside the row of giant machinery.

'Where do you think you're going?'

Jamie turned slightly in the semi-darkness as Logan's tall frame loomed up beside her. 'To bed,' she answered in a faintly puzzled voice.

Logan shook his head slowly from side to side. 'No dice, Jamie—you sleep in the caravan. Either you come of your own free will, or I carry you inside. The choice is yours.'

'Why?' she demanded in a low undertone. 'I fully intend locking all the doors. There won't be an opportunity for a repeat of last night.'

'Do you want to walk to the caravan, or shall I carry you?'

'I'll scream,' she threatened, and he laughed. 'I'll yell for Blake Curtis——'

'Blake already knows and approves, Jamie. He no more wants you to be harassed or frightened during your enforced stay among us than I do. Keeping the men on an even keel is his concern. Believe me, it's easier this way.'

Easier? She had to be out of her mind even to consider it! 'You're not serious?' she queried with intended sarcasm. 'We don't even like each other —five minutes together and we begin arguing.' A further thought occurred, one that made her angry. 'What connotation will the men place on me sharing your caravan?' She waved a hand in a gesture of angry frustration. 'I'll be darned if I'll be labelled as a—a——'

'Woman of easy virtue?' he prompted mockingly, and she had to restrain herself from physically hitting him.

'Yes—I mean *no*,' she finished furiously.

'In your own best interests, you'll trust me and do as you're told,' Logan advised bluntly. 'I intend smoking a cigarette, which will take all of five minutes. After that, I'm coming in. You'd be advised to get inside, change, and get into bed if you want to spare your blushes,' he concluded sardonically.

'You're a bully,' she snapped resentfully, adding for good measure, 'and a brute. No wonder you have a caravan to yourself—no one else could bear to put up with you!'

'Four minutes,' he reminded her tauntingly, standing there with his arms folded, so sure of himself she actually raised a hand to strike him. 'Oh no,' he reproved softly, catching hold of it in mid-air and applying just enough pressure to retain his grasp. 'Whether you go in there under duress or of your own free will is immaterial to me—so make up your mind.'

'I hate you!' she vouched steadily.

'Go right on hating me,' Logan drawled indolently. 'It won't cause me to lose any sleep, I assure you.'

With her head held high Jamie swept past him and mounted the single step into the caravan with as much dignity as she could muster. Never could she remember feeling so hopelessly angry—certainly not to a point of wanting to rage and scream like an uncontrollable, intractable child!

'Turn off the light when you change,' Logan's voice instructed from the doorway. 'Up until now there hasn't been the necessity for such civilised refinements as curtains.'

'If you expect me to don a frivolous concoction of nylon and lace, then you're doomed to disappointment,' she declared icily, and rummaged inside her bag until she found what she wanted. 'I embarked on a camping trip, not an attempt to dazzle any males who crossed my path. I intend sleeping in a blouse and jeans.'

'Hurry it up. You've a few scant minutes before I come in, then the light gets doused and we sleep. The men rise at dawn, breakfast, then hit the road. Right now, a chattering female isn't high on my list of priorities.'

The best policy was to remain silent, no matter how much he antagonised and provoked—she had all day tomorrow to think up some suitable pithy remarks with which to metaphorically slay him. The few seconds before she slipped into the vehicle that would ultimately take her away from here would be an ideal time. She'd have the last word yet!

To save vigorous brushing she quickly twisted her hair into a thick plait, tossed it back over her shoulder, then stepped into the jeans and undid her skirt.

She viewed the bunk with some misgiving, not at all sure she was wise to stay in the same caravan with someone like Logan. If he was a gentleman, she pondered with a grimace, he would allow her to sleep here alone and not insist on sharing——

A slight sound outside sent her scrambling hastily up on to the top bunk, and she lay with her face to the wall hardly daring to breathe as the screen door creaked open. It was too hot for bedcovers, and she lay supine, willing her tense muscles to relax as the door snapped shut.

There was a rustle of clothing being discarded, then the click of a switch and the caravan was plunged into darkness.

Every sound seemed to be magnified, and Jamie was made startlingly aware of Logan's presence as he settled his large frame comfortably. She became supremely conscious of every breath she took as her heart began to thud loudly in her breast, and cursed herself for being all kinds of a fool.

'Goodnight, Jamie,' Logan bade sardonically, his voice a cynical drawl, and she uttered a muffled response.

CHAPTER FOUR

JAMIE scanned the south-east horizon in an attempt to pick up a moving cloud of dust that would herald the arrival of her friends. It was late afternoon, and she felt as if she had been waiting for hours. The day had proceeded as an exact replica of the previous day, except possibly for the few short sentences she had exchanged with Logan at breakfast and at lunch. And now the waiting seemed interminable.

It was almost impossible to distinguish a moving object in the distance with so many heavy machines operating in the area, and after a while her eyes grew tired with the concentrated effort.

Sunday night she would be back in Alice Springs, and she couldn't help feeling disappointed that she had missed out on the trip to the Rock, for within a month she and Susan would begin moving south to Adelaide via rail, for the stretch of road between Alice Springs and Port Pirie was reputedly rough and the automobile club advised freighting all vehicles other than four-wheel-drive.

It was after five o'clock when a dusty well-loaded station wagon pulled into the compound sounding a triumphant burst of the horn, then doors slammed and voices joined in the noisy arrival.

'Susan!' Jamie flew across to the slightly-built blonde and hugged her tightly.

'You're okay?' Susan queried, her scrutiny intent as she stood back and surveyed her friend. 'You really had us worried—I was all for leaving yesterday, but we were assured you were in safe hands, and the boys wanted to make the most of the trip, especially as we'd come so far.'

Jamie gave a quick nod of agreement. 'Maybe I'll make it another time,' she dismissed lightly. 'Anyway, don't stand out here—come on in and have a cool drink. I've been given the use of a caravan during the day.'

'Man, that's the best offer I've had all day,' Michael declared with emphasis, and Jamie laughed as she indicated Logan's caravan.

'It's not much cooler inside, but at least there's screens on the windows and the door, so we shan't be pestered by these wretched flies.'

Both young men were in their early twenties, of medium height, and whereas Michael was fair, Richard sported dark hair and a well-developed beard. In Australia on an extended holiday, they had recently spent a few months working at Mount Isa and were due to leave for Darwin within a few days of arriving back in Alice Springs.

'You had this to yourself?' Richard queried idly as he stepped inside. 'How do they generate power out here? Ah—I see, butane gas. And supplies—I presume they're sent out with reasonable frequency?'

Jamie frowned, unable to recollect either Blake Curtis or Logan making any mention of how they received their supplies. 'I can't say for sure, but I imagine with fifteen or sixteen men to be fed, it would have to be fairly often.'

Michael glanced around the interior of the caravan with interest. 'My God, it's hot! Reckon our host will mind if we exchange some of our warm cans of beer for cold ones from his refrigerator?'

'I don't think so, as long as you leave him a few for tonight—by tomorrow the others will have chilled sufficiently,' Jamie explained, then turning towards Susan she begged with interest, 'Now, tell me what you thought of Ayers Rock.'

'In a word—magnificent, and well worth the trip,' Susan enthused, her bright features alive with enthusiasm. 'The colour changes at dawn and sunset have to be seen to be believed—they're incredible! And the caves, gulleys, and erosions in the rock itself—some of the rock drawings and paintings are really beautiful. Their stark simplicity enhances the graphic detail, and the guide we had was very good, explaining the significance as he translated what the drawings meant. Some of the stories were uncanny.'

'It was a shame you broke down,' Michael shrugged. 'But lucky that it was near here where help was on hand. Just imagine if it had been someplace else.'

'I had plenty of food and water,' Jamie responded carefully, not really caring for his nonchalant attitude. 'I could have survived for a week without undue discomfort. By then I would have been found— even if no other vehicle turned up, you were due to pass through on the way back to Alice Springs, so I would have been rescued.'

'Have you heard what's to happen about the vehicle you rented?' Susan queried, her friendly face creased with concern.

'They're sending someone out and it will be towed back to Alice Springs. Logan assures me the company exonerates me from any blame.'

'Logan?' Michael queried idly. 'Is he in charge of this outfit?'

'I don't think so—at least not entirely,' Jamie responded with a puzzled frown, for it had occurred to her more than once over the past few days that Logan had considerable authority. 'Blake Curtis is the senior foreman.'

'You slept in the station wagon and spent your days in here.'

It was a statement issued by way of logical conclusion, and she was loath to inform them to the contrary. 'It was kind of Logan to allow me the use of his trailer,' she explained carefully.

'What about meals—did you cook your own?'

'A cook is employed,' she said slowly. 'But Logan seems to fend for himself, except for the occasional meal he has in the kitchen-mess with the rest of the men.'

'Do all trailers have two berths?'

'Yes,' Jamie acceded ambiguously.

'You're being evasive, honey,' Michael decided, eying her through narrowed lids. 'You did sleep in the station wagon, didn't you?'

She felt vaguely resentful, and was reluctant to answer. There was nothing between them except friendship, and he had no right to question her so thoroughly.

'Does it matter where Jamie slept?' Susan intervened quickly, shooting her friend a speculative glance. 'We've taken several reels of film, Jamie—I'll put them in to be developed first thing Monday morning, and with luck they'll be back by the end of the week. Hey,' she said suddenly, her head moving to one side as she listened intently. 'What's that noise?'

'The machines heading in for the night,' Jamie told her as the distant rumble became more noticeable. 'The men will be here soon. If you want to wash, Susan, you'd better come with me, otherwise you won't get the opportunity until after dinner.'

'Right—lead the way,' the other girl directed brightly. 'I'll snatch up a change of clothes and a towel and be there in seconds.'

By the time Jamie re-entered Logan's trailer

the machines were already stationary in the compound, and she waited for Logan to join her so that she could effect the necessary introductions.

It wasn't until Susan appeared that she could complete the formality, and she glanced surreptitiously at each of her friends to judge their reaction. Logan was at his most urbane, and although he gave the appearance of being easygoing to the point of indolence, Jamie caught the swift intentness of his glance and knew that he had summed up and characterised each of her friends with lightning judgment. He possessed a shrewd analytical mind, and not for the first time she wondered why he was content doing heavy manual labour when he could be wielding power from behind an office desk.

After dinner the men, faced with two attractive females, were in their element. Logan was the quietest of all, preferring to listen rather than participate, and Jamie grew increasingly irritated as the evening wore on and Michael's attentions became more obvious.

At last the men made a move to retire, and when everyone had dispersed to their various sleeping quarters Jamie wandered with Susan to where Richard and Michael had pitched their tent.

'Come for a stroll?'

Jamie glanced towards Michael and shook her head. 'It's late, and we all need to get up at dawn to make an early start. Goodnight.'

'Where are you going?' he asked.

'To collect my bag,' she said quietly.

'Isn't it in your station wagon?' Michael queried a trifle querulously.

'No.'

'Then you did sleep with him!' Michael accused, and she drew in her breath in an effort to control the angry retort that rose to her lips.

'I occupied the top bunk in his caravan,' she said with as much calm as she could muster.

'I bet!' His sarcastic comment incensed her to a point where she could have thrown something at him.

'Oh—grow up, Michael!' she flung icily, and pivoting round she walked away, striding across the compound with anger evident in every taut muscle in her body.

'Well, what have we here?' Logan mused idly as she stormed inside and let the screen door bang behind her. 'Had a spat with the boy-friend already?'

Jamie sent him a venomous look. 'He's not my boy-friend.'

A mildly raised eyebrow arched itself, then descended, and his rugged features assumed cynical amusement. 'He didn't take kindly to the news that you've been sharing my caravan.'

'You could say that,' she said tightly, gathering up her bag and stuffing clothes into it without any care whatsoever.

'You intend sleeping in the station wagon with Susan?'

'Have you any objection?'

His glance was level. 'You'll be more comfortable here.'

'Oh, for heaven's sake!' she exploded emotively. 'Two dictatorial men I don't need! Neither one of you has the right to boss me around.' Her dark eyes flashed angrily. 'I need some fresh air—I'm going for a walk!'

'Not alone. Out of sight of this camp you could easily lose your sense of direction and become lost.'

'Right now I'd rather take my chances with the spinifex and the snakes!'

'That bad, hmm? Come on, then,' Logan directed

sardonically, unbending his lengthy frame from the couch and moving to stand beside her. 'I'm not averse to a bit of exercise.'

'I'd rather go alone,' she hurled ungratefully, and his mouth twisted into a wry smile.

'Either I come with you, or you don't go at all.'

Jamie just looked at him, then with an angry movement she swept past him and stepped outside. She didn't care which direction she took, it was enough to get as far away as possible, and she almost ran in her haste to put as much distance as she could between herself and the compound.

After a few minutes Logan's voice came quietly in the darkness. 'Ease up, Jamie. You want I should confront the man and explain?'

'You don't understand—I don't care about Michael. That's not it, at all.' She slowed down a little and made a gesture of hopelessness. 'It's just— everything, I guess. The heat, breaking down out here, not being able to make it to Ayers Rock. I desperately wanted to see it for myself, and now I guess I never will. Susan and I will only be in Alice Springs for another month, then we're heading down to Adelaide.' She looked up at him. 'Michael is just a friend, a fellow-New Zealander Susan and I met two months ago. He and Richard wanted to make the trip to the Rock, and it seemed sensible to have them along. They had their own tent and were prepared to pay their share of expenses. If Michael read more into it than that, then that's his mistake.'

'Then why worry about it?'

'I'm not. Oh, let's go back,' she uttered wretchedly. 'Susan won't be able to get to sleep until I settle my gear, and it's still in the caravan.'

'Just as you please.' His shrug was imperceptible in the darkness, and he paused to transfer a cigarette from its packet to his mouth, then a lighter flared, momentarily illuminating his compelling features, and Jamie was struck by the strength evident—the sheer physical force of the man.

Out here they seemed so alone, as if there were just the two of them. The camp could have been a hundred miles away, and she was aware of some intangible thread drawing them together. It almost made her catch her breath, and she had to physically refrain from reaching out and touching him.

It's crazy, she whispered silently. I don't even like the man, yet there's something magical in the air— a sensation of spirits weaving a spell over which I have no control. Time lay suspended, and she stood still, hardly daring to breathe as she waited for the moment to leave.

'I thought you wanted to go back,' Logan's voice interposed solemnly, yet there was a hint of sardonic amusement evident that brought her sharply out of her slightly dazed state.

'There's something about the Outback, isn't there?' she queried softly.

'Away from the madding crowds that haunt the concrete and steel jungle of the cities?'

'More than that. Elemental, and perhaps a little cruel. Providing the challenge of survival.'

'Profound thoughts, Jamie?' he mocked cynically, and she strained to catch his expression in the darkness.

'Why did you come here, Logan?' she asked.

'The spirit of adventure?'

'I find that difficult to believe,' she dismissed wryly. 'You dress the part, you even look the part behind the controls of that huge grader. But something doesn't quite click—I'm not sure what it is.'

'Perhaps I'm a fugitive from justice?' he mocked, and the absurdity of it brought a bubble of laughter bursting from her throat.

'I guess we'd better head back,' she suggested a few minutes later. 'Susan will be wondering where I am.'

'Not only Susan,' Logan declared indolently. 'It would appear your—friend has decided to investigate your whereabouts.'

Jamie turned, and in the gloom she could just discern a shape moving towards them. 'Oh—damn!' she swore inelegantly.

'You must have given him some encouragement.'

Indignation rose to the fore. 'I didn't—I haven't,' she vouched with a trace of anger, hating his mocking cynicism.

'Well, it would appear he seems to think so,' Logan drawled.

A dark shape loomed close, and Jamie could almost sense the anger emanating from Michael's lean frame.

'Jamie, what are you doing out here?' he demanded, his hand reaching out and catching hold of her arm. 'What's *he* doing with you?'

She tried to move away, and her efforts to set her arm free from his grasp proved fruitless. 'I felt like some fresh air,' she said coldly. 'Logan wouldn't allow me to walk out here alone.'

'You could have asked me.'

A sigh of exasperation left her lips. Men—you couldn't please them no matter what you did! 'You weren't around when I decided to leave the compound,' she said quietly, and sensed Logan's amusement at the situation. Darn him—he was far too perceptive! 'We were on our way back,' she explained. 'In any case, I didn't realise I would be missed.'

'Jamie.' Michael reached out and grasped hold of her hand, pulling her close, ignoring Logan completely. 'I thought you liked me,' he intoned softly. 'Why are you giving me the brush-off?'

Oh lord, she groaned silently. 'I'm not. I went for a walk, Michael, that's all.'

'With him.'

He made it sound like a mortal sin, and Jamie was astute enough to realise that other men would regard a man of Logan's calibre a threat to their own success with the opposite sex. He had the knack, whether intentional or not, of making other men in his presence pale into insignificance.

'Don't be ridiculous,' she dismissed. 'Logan merely came along as a precautionary measure.' She was supremely conscious of Logan beside her. It was impossible that he couldn't hear, despite the conversation being conducted in an undertone. If only he'd walk on, so that she could argue without having him overhear every word!

'Susan and Richard hit it off,' said Michael in an aggrieved voice. 'I thought you and I . . .'

'What did you think?' she demanded in a deadly quiet voice, fury building up inside her like a raging storm.

'That this trip would be an excellent opportunity for us to get to know one another better.'

Jamie drew a deep breath and prayed for patience. 'If you were fostering any ideas that I would be willing to share your tent—forget it! This trip was meant to be strictly a platonic arrangement, and you know it.' She turned away and moved quickly in the direction of the compound. 'Goodnight!' She broke into a run in her desire to put as much space between them as possible. If she didn't, she'd end up saying something regrettable, such was her anger with Michael for conducting what should have been a private conversation in Logan's hearing. Everything was going wrong—it was almost as if this trip had been fated from the very beginning!

Jamie opened the screen door of Logan's caravan and swept inside. With luck she'd be able to collect her bag and be out again before he came in. Right now she didn't trust herself to be civil, and the desire to give in to childish tears was almost undeniable.

Of all the crazy ideas! she fumed silently. Not once had she given Michael any encouragement. She crossed to the bunk, caught up her bag, and turned round to see Logan regarding her with an expression that was impossible to define.

'I'm on my way. Goodnight,' she bade tightly as she drew abreast of him, and she couldn't meet his eyes for the mockery she knew to be there. 'Please, Logan—let me pass.'

'Were you really naïve enough to embark on this trip totally unsuspecting that more was expected of you than just the sharing of expenses?' His voice was calm and held no hint of cynicism, and her eye lashes swept up.

'Yes,' she cried with righteous indignation 'We've known them for two months, and in tha time not once did he make a pass. How was I to know he was merely biding his time?'

'You're a very attractive young woman,' Logan drawled sardonically, crossing his arms across his chest as he looked down at her. 'Surely the possibility crossed your mind?'

'All right,' she conceded furiously, 'so maybe it did. I wasn't worried—I can handle myself. Besides, he's a New Zealander.'

'Good grief,' he returned wryly. 'You don't mean to say you thought that would protect you?'

Jamie glared up at him. 'I've done a specialised course in self-defence. He wouldn't have got very far.'

Logan began to laugh, softly at first, then his chest shook with it, so that it infuriated her beyond measure.

Without pausing for thought she lashed out at him, hitting him wherever she could, goaded to lengths that frightened her. She, Jamie Prentiss, who had never lost her temper in her life! Yet here she was behaving like some primitive she-cat. If only she could believe she was hurting him! But her blows fell against a chest that felt rock-hard beneath her fists, and she could have cried with frustration as he held her away. Her fingers dug into his arms, trying to bruise the flesh, but came into contact with hard muscle and sinew against which her puny strength could find no leverage.

'Hey, little girl—that's enough,' he cautioned hardily, shaking her slight figure to emphasise his words. 'I won't be your punching bag,' he warned. 'Keep it up, and I'm liable to get mad.'

'You amaze me,' she flung heatedly, her breath coming in short gasps. 'I thought you were invincible—the total chauvinistic misogynist!'

His eyes narrowed fractionally. 'Careful,' he advised. 'I warned you once before about your sassy tongue.'

'Is that a threat, Logan—or a promise?'

Anger leapt into those dazzling blue eyes, and she suddenly felt afraid of what she'd aroused.

'Maybe it's about time you found out,' he muttered softly, hauling her close.

'Logan——' her protest died on her lips as she caught sight of his expression, and she began to struggle against him, twisting in his arms as she tried desperately to evade his descending head.

Never had she been made so aware of a man's physical strength, and she was powerless to escape the hurtful pressure of his mouth as it plundered

hers, forcing her lips apart as he savaged the delicate
tissue against her teeth. Not content, he blazed a
ravaging exploration of her mouth, and when he
lifted his head she felt as if she would fall, her head
was so light that dizziness forced her to grasp hold
of his arms until the trailer walls stopped swirling
crazily.

Tears sprang up behind her eyes, the pupils dilat-
ing with fearful uncertainty as she gazed mutely into
his face.

'That wasn't quite fair,' he grimaced with a gesture of self-disgust. A muscle tensed along his jaw as
he glimpsed the tears welling in her eyes.

Jamie viewed him through a watery mist, unable
to move if her life depended upon it, and she gave
a convulsive shudder as he drew her body against
his. She felt his lips touch her hair, then his fingers
were beneath her chin, forcing it high. His lips
touched hers, gently, like the wings of a butterfly,
and a shaft of incredible pleasure shot through her
veins as he began a sensual trailing path from her
lips and down her neck. The effect was erotic, like
nothing she had ever experienced, and without
conscious thought she began to respond. Of their
own volition her arms crept up to encircle his
neck, and she stood on tiptoe to reach him, aware
within seconds that her feet no longer touched the
floor as he enfolded her slim body close against his
own.

How long it was before he put her down and held
her at arm's length she had no idea, for she had little
recollection of time.

'Go, Jamie,' Logan directed brusquely, and without a word she turned and ran—down the steps and
across the compound to the station wagon.

Safely inside, she opened up her sleeping-bag and
spread it out, then she eased her length on to it and

shifted quietly in an effort to get comfortable.

'What happened out there?' Susan questioned softly, and Jamie gave a sudden start.

'Not much,' she dismissed lightly. 'I went for a walk.'

'Is there something between you and Logan, or am I imagining things?'

'There's nothing,' she denied, aware that she should offer some explanation. 'I'm cross with Michael,' she said fiercely.

'Want to talk about it?'

Jamie lifted a hand to her bruised lips. 'Do you mind if we leave it until tomorrow? We should try to get to sleep.'

'Goodnight.'

Jamie murmured a response, her eyes wide open as she stared sightlessly ahead. She lay perfectly still, afraid to move lest she disturb Susan. A long shuddering breath tore through her body, and she closed her eyes in an effort to shut out the memory of Logan's punishing kiss. Remembering her response sent a wave of mortification warming her cheeks, and she uttered a thankful prayer that after bidding him a brief farewell in the morning she would never see him again.

Jamie and Susan rose at first light, swiftly rolling up their bedding, and as they washed and changed their clothes Richard and Michael took down the tent and stowed it on to the roof-rack on top of the station wagon prior to leaving.

Breakfast was a cup of coffee and some bread toasted over an open fire, and they had almost finished eating when the first of the men emerged from a nearby caravan.

At once Jamie began to urge the others to hurry, for she had no desire to face Logan—even though logic persuaded her that she would have to voice her thanks. Perhaps, she thought, Blake Curtis would put in an appearance first, and with luck they might be on their way, thus escaping a confrontation with Logan.

It was a slim hope, and of no avail, for minutes later Jamie glimpsed his tall frame moving purposely towards them. Blake Curtis was there, too, which didn't make it so bad, but there was no evading Logan as he drew abreast of the station wagon.

'You're ready?'

Jamie nodded, and Susan sparkled charmingly, her smiling manner more than making up for Jamie's lack of conversation.

'Take it easy on the way back,' Logan instructed, his eyes raking Jamie's slender form, but still she refused to meet his gaze.

'Well, I guess we'd better get on our way,' Susan declared, shooting her friend a curious glance. 'Thanks for your hospitality.'

'Thanks, Blake,' Jamie voiced carefully. 'I appreciate everything you've done, and I'm sorry if my presence created any inconvenience.'

His lopsided grin was reassuring. 'How could a pretty young slip of a thing like you be an inconvenience? My dear, the morale among my men was never so high!' He extended a tanned well-calloused hand. 'Have a good trip, and all the best for your future travels.'

'Thanks,' Jamie smiled sunnily, deliberately excluding the tall figure beside him. 'Well, I guess we'd better go before the sun gets much higher. It'll be hot enough later on. 'Bye, and thanks once again.' She turned and slid into the front passenger seat, closed the door behind her and willed the others to follow her example. It had already been decided that Susan would drive until midday, when they would stop for lunch, then Richard would take over.

Mercifully the others were conscious of the need to get away, and within minutes the station wagon eased forward and moved out from the compound with a series of horn blasts and much arm-waving.

A silent sigh escaped Jamie's lips. Thank goodness they were on their way, each mile taking them further away from the man she had decided was the most hateful male she'd ever encountered. Self-assured and thoroughly impossible, she added for good measure. If she never set eyes on him again, it would be too soon! In a matter of two days he had turned her orderly world upside down, made her startlingly aware that she had never really been properly kissed before, and had rendered her un-awakened emotions into a state of turmoil. She should be glad—yes, *glad*, she would never see him again. If she'd stayed another day ... heaven knows what could have happened. Undoubtedly she was just another female in a long line of women who queued for his attention. Someone he could make use of, then discard when it suited him. Fate had been kind in rescuing her from certain heartache, she assured herself silently. He probably wouldn't give her another thought.

'You're very quiet, Jamie,' Susan murmured as she glanced across the space between them, concern on her friendly features.

'I'm fine,' Jamie responded quickly, giving a bright smile that dazzled. 'Just a bit tired, that's all.'

'There's some Disprin if you've a headache. Shall I stop?'

'No—really.' Heavens, she'd have to perk up a bit, otherwise Susan would begin to suspect something was amiss and begin questioning, and she didn't want that!

'What are our chances of making it through to Alice Springs tonight?' Michael queried, and both girls exchanged a doubtful glance.

'I won't drive after dark,' Susan admitted frankly. 'I guess we could get there before dusk if we don't take too much time out for lunch.'

'Ugh—who'd want to stop for longer than we have to?' he offered, his features assuming distaste. 'The flies eat us alive within seconds of the car becoming stationary. How they scent us so quickly I'll never know.'

'In another hour it will be so hot,' Richard declared. 'Imagine living out here in these conditions —hardly any rainfall for years, no real amenities. Just endless miles of red dust, heat, and wretched flies.'

'It's not that bad,' Jamie found herself saying, thinking of Blair and Jill Frazer and their comfortable homestead.

'Isolation, not another soul for miles—you'd have to be joking!' Michael declared scathingly.

'It takes a sturdy breed to accept near-desert conditions,' she defended. 'Determination, and the challenge it provides, would suit very few.'

'Turn on the radio—let's catch the news.'

After that the miles seemed to fly, and the terrain remained unchanging. The sun rose high in the sky, beating down to earth with an almost unbearable heat, which combined with the dust that seeped into the vehicle and the flies which converged en masse whenever they drew to a halt, tended to fray even the mildest of tempers.

It was a tremendous relief to get on to the sealed strip of bitumen on the outskirts of Alice Springs, and to see the first signs of civilisation again. With-

in minutes they were entering the main street where
they unloaded Richard and Michael's gear, bade
them farewell, then Jamie drove on to the apartment
at the other end of town.

Unpacking was achieved in the minimum of time,
and by mutual consent they elected to leave hosing
down the station wagon until the following day. A
meal of sorts, just an omelette and a salad, followed
by fruit, then both girls showered and clambered
into bed, too tired to do more than offer each other a
brief goodnight before settling down to sleep.

CHAPTER FIVE

WITHIN a few days it seemed as if Jamie had never been away, and her encounter with Logan and the road-gang slipped into the background as life assumed its usual day-to-day pattern.

The hotel was busy, peaking at midday and again in the evening, at times so hectic she scarcely had time to think.

After two months of serving behind the bar she had become adept at drawing beer, and could hold several glasses in one hand beneath the tap. No longer were the different sized glasses a mystery, for she knew a schooner from the smaller middy, and was well used to being requested to add a dash of sarsaparilla, ginger ale, lemonade, or stout to the beer. She was even becoming accustomed to the many strange accents of the new Australians among the clientele, and she didn't have to request many to repeat their order. Being a 'new hand' no longer applied, as she had become accepted by one and all.

In a way, she would miss the friendly atmosphere, she decided pensively. It had been fun, and something different. Returning to city life and sitting behind an office desk would seem deadly dull by comparison. However, she and Susan had come to Australia to travel its length and breadth, and there was still a considerable amount of the vast continent they had to see. A few more weeks in Alice Springs and they would leave, put the station wagon on the train down to Port Pirie, then drive to Adelaide where with luck they would be able to find accommodation and a job without too much delay. Three months in Alice Springs had provided them with sufficient money with which to traverse yet another leg of their journey.

Friday morning dawned hot and dry, not unlike the days preceding it, and there was nothing to warn Jamie that it would turn out to be any different. She was due to report to the hotel at two in the afternoon, and would work until ten on an unbroken shift.

There was a farewell party for Michael and Richard tonight and she supposed she would have to go, although as the afternoon wore on she began to view thoughts of a cool shower followed by bed and a good book with considerable favour.

The bar was crowded, packed in with men attempting to quench their thirst and socialise with their mates, and business was hectically brisk to a point where she began to wish she possessed two pairs of hands. Her smile became a conscious effort, and she would have given anything to be able to rest her feet even for a minute. Yet there was still an hour to go before closing time, and then it would be at least a further fifteen minutes or so before she could leave.

'Yes—what would you like?' she queried mechanically as she moved towards the next customer.

'A schooner, Jamie,' a familiar voice drawled, its deep faintly sardonic tones distinctive.

Logan! Her heart skipped a beat, then began racing as she assimilated the shock of seeing him again. Carefully she schooled her features into an expression of pleasant surprise.

'Hello,' she greeted with a smile. 'You're a long way from the road-gang.' Deftly she took a glass and filled it, thankful for two months of practice that ensured she served the beer with a minimum head. She placed it on the counter in front of him, extracted the correct money from the coins he placed there, transferring them into the cash register.

Conscious of several other men requiring service close by, Jamie moved on to serve them, but she was aware of Logan standing back from the bar and moving further down to the end of the counter where he remained until the bar closed. No matter what she did she sensed him watching her, until she felt she would scream if he didn't leave. It had the effect of making her quiet to the point where several regular customers asked if something was wrong, and she had to make a conscious effort to smile and joke, for this was what they expected.

If only Logan would leave she could relax, but he seemed to take pleasure in idly filling in his time, drinking his beer slowly and with evident enjoyment. She wanted to ask what he was doing in Alice Springs, particularly here in this hotel when he could drink elsewhere. It was crazy to feel as if she was a mouse being watched over by a rather superior cat, but she did, and after an hour it became obvious that he had no intention of moving until the bar closed.

Jamie surreptitiously observed him talking to Susan on more than one occasion, and she wondered what they could possibly be talking about. At closing time he was one of the last to leave, although after waiting so long for him to go she missed the actual moment of his departure.

'Phew—at long last!' Jamie breathed thankfully as the publican closed the side door, and Susan gave a sigh that defied description.

'Right, let's get these glasses out of the way,' Susan began with methodical briskness. 'You do the counter, and I'll begin on this lot. With luck we'll be out of here in under ten minutes. Then it's home for a quick shower and a change of clothes. By ten-thirty we should be at the party.'

Party—how could she have forgotten about it? 'Oh lord!' she groaned aloud. 'Susan, I'm so tired —my feet ache, and I'm about as enthusiastic at going out as a wet dishmop. All I want to do is to fall into bed.'

'Jamie, you've got to come,' Susan wailed as she stacked glasses into the dishwasher. 'Besides, I've asked Logan. He's taking us.'

Cold anger clutched at Jamie's stomach and squeezed it painfully. 'You did what?'

Susan had the grace to look nonplussed. 'He seemed to be standing there with not much to do. I thought he might like to come. We know him, and besides, what's one more guest?' she queried defensively. 'You don't mind, do you?'

What could she say? But yes, she did mind, very much.

Logan was standing outside the side entrance when she emerged with Susan some ten minutes later, and Jamie felt her nerve-ends curl alarmingly at the sight of him. She wanted to run and hide, but that wasn't possible, and she cursed whatever it was that brought him to Alice Springs.

She wanted to talk to him naturally, exchange a smile and treat him as a friend, but how could she when his mere presence tied her tongue in knots and made her feel about as poised as a teenager about to embark on a first date?

Logan followed them to the flat in his vehicle, a slightly dusty Land Rover, and once inside he took a seat at Susan's indication, choosing a large armchair in the lounge while Jamie and Susan took turns for the shower.

Jamie found herself stalling for time as she applied her make-up, and twice she entertained the idea of excusing herself on the grounds of a headache. Only the knowledge that such an excuse would draw Logan's mocking cynicism prevented her from voicing it. She wished with all her heart that he hadn't chosen to reappear now when she had just begun not to think of him constantly.

'Jamie, come on!' Susan called. 'It's nearly quarter to eleven.'

Well, there was nothing else for it but to go out there with a smile on her face and attempt to play the part of a charming guest. If Logan dared to regard her with amusement she'd hit him!

The dress she wore accented her slim curves and was delightfully feminine, its deep gold lending her hair a rich burnished hue which contrasted with her tanned limbs. A deep vee neckline exposed a generous cleavage, although the cut was deceptive, for on closer inspection it was more demure than first supposed. Slim-heeled sandals gave a touch of elegance, and she emerged into the lounge feeling confident and ready to tackle Logan.

Jamie rode in the front seat, with Susan seated on the outside, and during the short journey she was aware of the faintly saturnine enigmatic man behind the wheel in a way that made her veins course with liquid fire.

The party was well under way when they arrived, and Jamie did her best to slip away from Logan's side and thus elude his company after the initial introductions were effected, but wherever she went he seemed to be not more than a few feet distant.

It wasn't as if he talked to her, he was just *there* —tall, broad, and exuding virile masculinity from every nerve and fibre. His expression was inscrutable whenever she glanced his way, and she was supremely conscious of his every move, so much so that it inhibited her natural spontaneity.

The music was loud, alternating between disco

and rock, and almost everyone was dancing—or attempting to in the limited space available. The air was thick with tobacco fumes, which combined with the noise was beginning to give her a headache. She would have given anything to be able to abandon herself to the party spirit. Maybe it was a combination of too many late nights, arduous working hours, not to mention the presence of a man she had thought never to set eyes upon again.

For the third or fourth time—she'd lost count—she shook her head and smilingly refused yet another request to dance. Soon she would have to participate, otherwise it would become noticeable, and she preferred to remain as inconspicuous as possible.

'Dare I ask?' a deep voice drawled from behind. 'Or will I too join the ranks of the unaccepted?'

Jamie turned and looked up into the mocking blue eyes so far above her own, and she considered him thoughtfully. 'What are you doing here, Logan?' she managed calmly. 'Not in Alice Springs, but *here*, in this room?'

'Would you believe—to see you?'

'Why?' she asked baldly, and saw a gleam of amusement lift the corners of his wide mouth.

'Well, I could declare myself smitten by your—er——' he paused deliberately, glancing at the exposed cleft of her bosom, then went on to finish lazily—'charms. However, the truth, Jamie—I'm flying down to Ayers Rock by private charter at first light tomorrow. There's a spare seat on the plane if you'd like it.'

Unwilling to build up her hopes, she queried cautiously, 'Are you going alone?'

A slight smile lifted the corner of his mouth. 'No, a photographer by the name of Jake Templeton will be along for the ride.'

'When do you intend coming back?'

'Sunday.'

The temptation to accept was very great. 'Where would I sleep?' An innocent enough question, but one she had to settle.

'Not with me,' Logan drawled. 'I don't seduce children.'

Jamie let her gaze rove over his features, noting the finely etched lines at the outer corners of his eyes, the deep crease that ran vertically from jaw to cheekbone. At a guess, he was in his mid-thirties, perhaps a year or two more.

'You'll be quite safe—you have my word,' he vouchsafed brusquely. 'Yes or no?'

He really couldn't care less, she decided wryly. Well, if she didn't go she would never have the opportunity again. 'I'll come,' she agreed cautiously. 'What time, and where?'

'Be ready at six. I'll collect you.'

'What about food?' If necessary she could forage among the cupboards in the flat, for there was sure to be something suitable she could take.

'All taken care of, Jamie,' he assured her, and he drained the contents of his glass and set it down on a nearby table. 'Now, how about that dance?'

He didn't give her the chance to refuse, and it wasn't until she was in his arms among the crush of people that she remembered she hadn't actually consented to partner him.

Being close to Logan was a heady experience, and she was sure her pulse accelerated to an alarming rate. He had the power to render her bones to jelly, and she kept her lashes lowered for fear of what he might read in her eyes. It was sheer madness, a madness that could bring only heartache—hers. She was under no illusion that her reaction was one-sided.

It was ten minutes before he relinquished his

hold—ten minutes of sheer bliss, where nothing seemed to touch them.

'You need to be bright-eyed and bushy-tailed if you're to make the most of your time at Ayers Rock,' Logan slanted as he led her away from the centre of the room. 'Unless you particularly want to stay here, I'd advise leaving soon to allow a few hours' sleep before dawn. Susan looks set to remain for quite a while yet. Want me to drop you off at the flat?'

It was already after midnight, and even allowing time to push a few clothes into an overnight bag in the morning, there were only five hours left in which to sleep. 'Thank you. Give me a few minutes to explain to Susan,' Jamie asked, searching the room quickly, catching sight of her friend deep in conversation with Richard.

Susan's quick smile and wicked wink indicated what she thought of Logan's invitation, and Jamie found herself shaking her head in emphatic denial.

'Enjoy yourself,' Susan bade, adding impishly, 'He's a gorgeous hunk of masculinity, Jamie. Half your luck!'

'I could be fair, fat and forty, for all the notice he takes,' Jamie responded dryly, and Susan laughed.

'Don't you believe it,' she reiterated softly.

Jamie pondered her friend's words during the short drive back to the flat, and when Logan brought the vehicle to a halt she sat quiet and still, almost afraid of what might come next.

'Goodnight, Jamie.' There was a faint mocking inflection in the impersonal directive, and she unclasped the door and slid out, unsure afterwards whether or not she had returned his salutation.

Even at six-thirty in the morning the sky was clear, a pale nondescript blue that contrasted sharply with the surrounding terrain. Below them stretched mile upon mile of dry red-brown earth, relieved only by clumped mulga and spinifex. The interior of the small Cessna was comfortably fitted out, and Jamie tried not to let her thoughts wander to the question that sprang to mind—why Logan had asked her to come along. Could it be that he had remembered her desire to see the giant monolith? Or was it possible he had organised the trip with her in mind? With a mental grimace she dismissed the latter—they weren't exactly compatible, and although she was conscious of the electricity between them, it was doubtful it was a two-way current! Logan presented the image of a hard-bitten, self-assured, and at times arrogant, man. She had as much chance of taming him as she had of bringing a jungle animal meekly to heel. Not, she assured herself hastily, that she wanted him—life with such a man would be impossible. Impossible, a tiny voice taunted, but never dull.

She glanced across the space separating them, endeavouring to discover some elusive trait in that chiselled profile. But she could find nothing, no hint of weakness that might allow her to suppose he could be a wolf in sheep's clothing.

Just then he turned, meeting her clear-eyed gaze with dazzling blue-chipped clarity, and it was she who dropped her lashes and looked away, missing his faint smile, and with a need to provide some conversation she mentioned the first thing that entered her head.

'All that white sand,' she began, pointing towards the ground far below the cockpit window. 'Is it an optical illusion?' She adjusted her sunglasses, transferring them down from their resting place on top of her head, for the glare from the rising sun hurt her eyes.

'Salt and gypsum, Jamie. Beneath the midday sun the surface shimmers and dances with mirages.' He leaned close, and she had to force herself to breathe evenly, grateful for the huge lenses of her sunglasses that hid her eyes. 'That's Lake Amadeus—it looks quite spectacular from the air, like a fine powdery snow. Perhaps that's why it's so arresting in an area where one is accustomed to seeing thousands of square miles of nothing but barren desert.' He moved back fractionally in his seat. 'You should see the desert after a winter rainfall—yes, it does rain occasionally,' he smiled. 'On the shady side of the sand ripples the desert ephemerals germinate, grow, flower and die in a matter of days. Delicate and transient, they're one of nature's floral miracles. Sturt's desert pea provides a carpet of colour, and the sandhills abound with white and yellow daisies. Then there's the cream, lemon and scarlet of the dwarf banksias and hakeas. Even the husky spinifex puts out green horns. And the air comes alive with birdlife, especially at dusk—pink and grey galahs, cockatoos, and the crested pigeons.'

Surprise lightened her attractive features as she turned to look at him. 'Why, Logan!' she teased. 'For all that harsh exterior, you have quite a poetical way with words.'

Eyes of vivid blue held hers. 'Out here one is made aware of the meaning of man's worth on earth, the mysterious beginnings of life itself,' he returned quietly, without a trace of mockery. 'All of God's creatures equal in the fight for survival. Simplicity, stark and cruel. It's almost possible to forget there's another world beyond the desert's fringe—the concrete and steel jungle of man's civilisation.'

Jamie swallowed convulsively as she felt the magnetic pull of his brand of charisma, a potent chemical reaction that was purely of the senses, part physical, enmeshed, so that it became almost a tangible thing. It was frightening to discover that one man alone held her destiny, and she could have wept with the futility of it. Somehow she had to survive the next two days without letting him guess the effect he had upon her. No matter how dearly it cost her, she would have to smile and act the cool unruffled companion.

'Your friend is very quiet,' she ventured in a desperate bid to place the conversation on a more prosaic level, and Logan uttered a soundless laugh.

'Jake won't come alive for at least another hour—he's no lark, more of a night-owl. I practically had to drag him out of bed this morning.'

'He's brought along an impressive amount of photographic equipment. There's no doubt about his intention,' she found herself voicing, and the man beside her let his features assume an expression of mocking indolence.

'Curiosity, thy name is woman,' he said softly, and she looked away, unable to hold his gaze.

Jamie caught sight of the giant monolith long before the small twin-engined plane began its circling descent, and she summoned to mind all that she had gleaned from tourist brochures and geographical books. The world's greatest single rock formation, rising to a height of one thousand one hundred and forty-three feet above its base, with a circumference of nearly six miles, it was known to the aboriginals as *Uluru*. From land so flat it rose with majestic beauty, like something thrust up from a prehistoric era, and as they drew close the vast gulleys and erosions stood out, throwing an ever-changing pattern of shadows that shaped and sharpened its symmetry.

Then the plane was taxiing to a halt close to the rock itself, dwarfed into insignificance, and Jamie followed Logan's example by undoing her seatbelt.

The air outside hit them with the force of a miniature furnace, and Jamie felt the perspiration begin to bead across her forehead. Soon she would become accustomed to the rapid rise in temperature, the change that was so great in the first few hours after dawn.

Logan and Jake preceded her from the plane, and she took the hand Logan extended in assistance to ground level. Idly she stood by as the two men reached inside and unloaded their equipment, then the engines roared, throttling back as the tiny plane slipped forward, then turned and began moving smoothly along the flat surface.

Jamie picked up her overnight bag and slung its strap over her shoulder, then caught up her sleeping-bag. 'Can I help you with anything?'

The glance Logan spared her held amusement. 'Your offer is appreciated, but no, Jake and I can manage.' He looked down at her feet. 'I'm glad to see you're wearing sensible shoes.'

She pulled a face at him. 'What did you expect? Stiletto heels? Like the girl scout, I came prepared.'

'Sunscreen cream, insect repellant, salt tablets, and a spare hand to wave away the flies?' Jake mocked, laughing openly as the first of a swarm zeroed in on them. 'Flies by day, and mosquitoes by night. God, I had to be mad to dream up this assignment!'

'You were born and bred out here,' Logan drawled laconically. 'Who else would they send?'

'Which is precisely why I escaped to the city just as soon as I was able to fly,' Jake retorted ruefully. 'No pun intended,' he grinned across at Jamie, who returned the smile with one of her own.

'Let's get this gear across to the camping ground,' Logan suggested, effortlessly lifting a heavy rucksack into the rear of a dusty Land Rover that minutes before had slid to a halt nearby. Jake did likewise with a similar pack, then followed it with a carton of provisions and a large cooler.

Once seated inside the Land Rover the driver introduced himself as the Park Ranger, then he swung the dusty vehicle around and drove away from the airstrip.

Jamie noted with surprise that there were a total of three motels, a chalet, and a visitors' centre all within a short distance of the camping area, and by the time the vehicle came to a halt she could feel the sweat running down the centre of her spine and in the valley between her breasts.

'This time of year most everyone is trying to escape the heat,' Jake voiced cynically. 'With my luck I get to spend a week in one of the hottest strips of land this side of the black stump!'

'Well, let's get the tent set up, our gear stowed inside, then we can cool off with a can of beer,' Logan decided with an unsympathetic grin, and Jamie tried to conceal her surprise.

Tent? She was to share a tent with Logan and Jake? Sleeping less than as few feet distant from both of them?

'Relax—it's a very versatile piece of equipment,' Logan told her. 'Mosquito and fly-proof, it's light and easy to assemble. You'll be amazed,' he ended mockingly.

With a wry flash of humour Jamie conceded silently that she had already shared a trailer with him—what could be so different in sharing a tent?

'Can I help?' She felt she had to ask, even though her offer would doubtless be brushed aside.

'Later, Jamie,' Logan dismissed, and without further ado he bent down and began untying the tapes around the bulky bundle he had dropped to the ground only minutes before. 'At the end of the day you can play cook. When this is set up, we'll get something to eat by way of a late breakfast, then we'll set off for a few hours. There's some sandwiches in the cooler, fruit juice and beer. We'll pack what we need into a rucksack.'

Obviously he didn't intend to waste any time, Jamie perceived. There was a lot to see, and she for one didn't want to sit around camp all day. She wanted to explore! Idly she watched as the tent began to unfold, and when it was securely staked it looked larger than she had first imagined was possible. Inside, quite roomy and comfortable—even spending a week or two under such conditions would be no hardship.

In no time at all Logan and Jake had hefted their gear beneath the lightweight canvas, and a glance at her watch determined that it was after nine—indeed time for a snack, especially as she had had little more than a quickly-gulped cup of coffee more than three hours ago.

'Okay, what will it be? Coffee?' Logan queried, then added a trifle sardonically, 'Or do Kiwis follow the British habit and indulge in tea? There's a thermos of hot water, sachets of instant coffee, or teabags—help yourself.'

'I'll get it,' she determined evenly, kneeling down beside the carton he had just opened. 'Jake, what will you have?' she queried, glancing up at him, then without turning her head, 'Logan?'

'Coffee, black, strong, and two sugars,' Logan answered, adding, 'There's powdered milk in there somewhere.'

'Likewise, black,' Jake declared. 'Three sugars,' he grinned, unabashed. 'I need the energy.'

Deftly Jamie set out mugs, spooned in sugar, and tore open the coffee sachets, then poured in the hot water and took out a spoon.

'Sandwiches will have to suffice for now,' Logan drawled, opening the cooler. 'We'll aim at having a good feed tonight.' He took the mug Jamie held out, and as their fingers brushed together he slanted her an amused glance, as if he was aware of the effect he was having on her.

Jamie was darned if she was going to give him the satisfaction of seeing her blush! She could hardly ignore him, but she could direct most of her attention towards Jake. Silently she handed Jake his coffee, offering a bright smile as she did so.

'Tell me about your photographic assignment. Do you operate independently, or are you under contract to a newspaper?'

'Freelance, Jamie. This particular venture will provide glossy plates for a pictorial book geared to encourage tourists to visit the Outback.' He grinned across at her and raised a quizzical eyebrow. 'Fancy vying with the scenery? If any of the males reading it get the idea there's any more women like you out here they'll book all the available tours in advance!'

Jamie laughed and shook her head. 'Sandwich?' She undid a sealed packet and held it out. It was good to be able to eat without being inundated with flies. A thought occurred as she bit into a thick meat sandwich—the food, her seat on the plane—she must approach Logan about paying her share. She didn't want to be beholden to him for anything.

'Right, let's get moving,' said Logan, standing to his feet in one fluid movement. 'We want to make as much as possible of the morning before the sun gets too hot.' He speared Jamie with an inscrutable glance. 'You did bring a hat?'

Her eyes lifted and settled on that proud nose, unwilling to rise any further, and she smiled sweetly at his left cheekbone. 'Of course. And I smothered every inch of exposed skin with cream—I've brought it along to carry with me for repeated applications throughout the day. As you can see, I'm wearing jeans and a long-sleeved shirt—thus observing the cover-up rule as against baring all beneath the midsummer sun.' She couldn't help the twinkle that lit her eyes mischievously alive. 'All present and accounted for, sir.' With a mock salute she slipped to her feet, grabbed up a rucksack and hitched it on to her shoulders, then twisted the length of her hair up beneath her hat and adjusted her sunglasses down on to her nose. 'Ready when you are!'

Logan's eyes darkened fractionally. 'That sassy tongue will get you into trouble yet,' he mocked quietly, and Jake emitted a roar of suppressed mirth.

'What's with you two? Is it open war, or just the way you react to each other?'

'Why, Jake,' Jamie began with mock seriousness, 'whatever gives you that idea?'

'A few hours beneath the heat of the sun, at the pace we set,' Logan drawled sardonically, 'and she'll cry for mercy.'

Jamie wrinkled her nose at him. 'And to think I wanted to come along!'

'I promised you a trip to the Rock, pint-size—not an invitation to a picnic. Now, are you ready, or must we stay here all morning arguing? And,' he cautioned softly, 'don't say "yes, sir" again. Jake's presence won't bother me a whit, I promise you.'

'I stand suitably rebuked—Logan,' she murmured with assumed docility. If he wanted to be a bear, he could jolly well be one—she was going to enjoy herself, even if it meant sunburn, mosquito bites, and being in a permanent state of frustration with the droves of flies that would hound them throughout the day!

His glance hinted darkly at retribution, but she deliberately dismissed it and concentrated on seeing as much as she could of her surroundings.

As they walked Jamie quickened her steps to keep abreast of the two men, who being a good twelve inches taller took longer strides and appeared to be strolling along with ease. She was young and fit, and if they could stand the heat and the pace, then so would she—even if it killed her!

Fortunately Jake stopped every ten minutes or so to set up a shot with his camera, and Jamie deliberately ignored the occasional glance Logan cast her, silently enquiring if she was tired or enervated by the growing heat.

'Have a drink,' he advised quietly when they had stopped for about the fifth time, and she stiffened her shoulders to refuse. 'Little, and often, Jamie—as against one long draught of liquid. We're almost to the caves. We'll head back to camp at midday, and take a siesta. After an early evening meal we'll walk right round the Rock. In the morning we'll climb to the top—a good pre-breakfast exercise to work up an appetite.' His grin was without mockery, and she found herself smiling back.

'I thought I was acclimatised to this heat,' she offered ruefully, sweeping a hand across her face for what seemed to be the thousandth time to ward off the flies.

'You picked the worst time of year to play tourist,' he told her. 'May through to September is best— when the outdoor temperatures are warm and mild.'

'It would have meant staying on in Townsville an extra three months,' she explained. 'Time we couldn't really afford if we were to be in Adelaide by the beginning of March.'

'You're keeping to some sort of time schedule?'

Jamie glanced up at him seriously. 'We want to leave for Perth by October, and we need at least six months to save sufficient money for expenses."

'And after Perth—where next?'

'Melbourne, then home, I guess.'

'No further plans to travel—England, Europe?'

She shaded her eyes from the intense sunlight, even the tinted lenses she wore did little to shade the glare. 'Maybe in a year or two,' she answered. 'It's two years since I saw my parents. After travelling around so long it will be nice just to stay in one place among familiar surroundings for a while.'

'You're very attached to them?'

'They're two very dear people,' Jamie said softly. 'Dad retired last year, and together they're sharing a lot more of each other's time. They don't like me being away, and I miss them very much.'

'No brothers or sisters?'

She shook her head. 'I came as something of a surprise quite late in their life when they'd all but given up hope of ever having a child.'

'So you were horribly spoiled as a consequence,' he commented cynically.

'No!' she flashed with indignation. 'Indulged on occasion, but Dad is old Army stock—spare the rod and spoil the child. I can assure you I received my share of chastisement.'

'Hmm,' Logan smiled, amusement gleaming darkly as he regarded her. 'Shall we continue?'

Now it was her turn to direct a few pertinent questions, she decided. 'What about your family, Logan? Presumably you have one somewhere? A wife, perhaps?'

His soft laughter reached her ears. 'No wife,

Jamie. As yet I haven't found the need to settle down with any one woman.'

'Of course—I should have known! You're a misogynist.'

'No. Let's just say I've developed a wariness of the opposite sex,' he mocked.

'Why, Logan?' she queried sweetly. 'Did some female break your heart way back in your past?'

'Shall we head towards the caves?' he countered with bland imperturbability.

Well, that was that, she thought ruefully. She was still none the wiser—except that he wasn't married. She was almost afraid to dwell on it in case her mind began to run away with her, and that would never do! Cool, calm and collected she must remain if she was to stay sane! He bothered her a mite too much already for her peace of mind.

'This cave is known as Women's Cave,' Logan told her a short while later as they paused beside the aperture. 'The aboriginals refer to it as *Djuga-jabbi*. Further round on the sun side are the wall paintings.'

The caves were a place of wonder, drawings and paintings on the rock so old, yet graphic in their own way, and if one studied them carefully it was possible to decipher the story they told.

CHAPTER SIX

IT was after six o'clock when they left camp and set out on foot to cover the six miles around the Rock. The intense heat had subsided a little, but even so it was still hot enough to get sunburnt. The flies were still as active as ever, and seemed doubly persistent. Jamie began to see the sense of a sunhat with netting that covered the face and neck, or one with corks bobbing from innumerable strings attached to its brim—just the type caricatured in cartoons, and to think she'd laughed at the time! It was far from being funny.

'Hey, Jamie,' Jake's voice intervened, and she glanced round at him to see that he stood with his camera poised and ready. 'Smile—be part of the background, honey.'

She pulled a face, then grimaced when she realised he'd taken the shot. 'Horror!' she accused with a grin.

'Well,' he warned, 'I did tell you to smile prettily.' He wound on the film, then focussed the lens. 'This time be serious.'

Jamie struck a pose, hoping as she laughed that she wouldn't swallow a fly. 'If I'd known you wanted a model, I'd have brought along some feminine clothes,' she teased. 'In jeans and blouse, my hair bunched up beneath my hat, who could tell whether I'm male or female?'

'There are a few subtle differences,' Logan drawled, his eyes settling on two of them, and when he lifted his gaze to meet hers the expression evident there sent a blush warming her cheeks.

'There's no doubting you're a girl, Jamie,' Jake chuckled. 'Now, another one. Take off your hat for a minute, and let all that gorgeous hair flow down over your shoulders. That's the girl,' he commended with approval. 'Now, swing your head— that's it. And again. Great! Smile up at Logan,' he directed. 'And you, you great hulk,' he grinned, 'look adoring, as a boy-friend would, huh?'

The camera clicked several times in succession, then Jamie was free of the encircling arm that had dropped about her shoulders, and Logan's chuckle echoed tantalisingly long after they had covered several hundred yards.

The shadows were beginning to lengthen, providing shade as they set a leisurely pace, and after a while they were walking through a dense growth of mulga.

'Are there many snakes around here?' Jamie couldn't help the query as it sprang to her lips. Like all non-Australians she had a healthy respect for reptiles, particularly the poisonous species. Perhaps coming from a country which had none made her more aware of them. She had seen several in zoos and sanctuaries, but she didn't fancy coming face-to-face with one in its natural habitat unless she could help it!

'Some,' Logan replied laconically. 'On the whole they slither out of sight at the slightest noise—unless you happen to come between them and their young. If they feel threatened, they'll strike.'

'You're trying to frighten me,' she accused ruefully, and saw his silent laughter. Oh, he was a callous brute!

'Not true,' he decried mildly. 'They're here, make no mistake. But you'll be fortunate if you get a glimpse of one.'

'Fortunate? That kind of luck I can do without!'

His humour was evident in the slight twist at the edges of his mouth. 'Don't fret,' he bade sardonically. 'Why do you suppose I insisted you wear shoes instead of open sandals, and jeans instead of shorts? If you do get bitten, I've a snakebit kit on hand.' His eyes teased her and she could cheerfully have hit him. 'I wouldn't let you die.'

'You're perfectly horrible!' she managed quietly, and he laughed out loud.

'Leave her alone, Logan,' Jake put in. 'You're an unmerciful sort of a guy, and she's too nice to tease.'

Logan looked down at her, and she refused to meet his gaze. 'Are you nice, Jamie?' he provoked. 'Or does that pretty exterior hide the deviousness of a cunning witch?'

Anger burned in her breast. Carefully schooling her features, she glanced upwards. 'Do you take pleasure from picking on someone half your size? In a fight, you'd win with one hand tied behind your back. But in a conflict of the mind I'd meet you on equal terms, and I'd make sure you didn't have the satisfaction of winning.'

There was a brief silence, explosive, and the atmosphere between them became charged with tension both mental and physical for a few brief seconds before it was broken by the sound of Jake's laughter.

'Bravo, Jamie! For once Logan has come up against someone who answers back. It must make a change from all those simpering city types you usually escort!'

'Do women simper over you, Logan?' she queried sweetly, fluttering her lashes in a gesture of deliberate provocation. 'My, my—is that so?' She considered him thoughtfully, then slowly shook her head. 'There's just no accounting for taste.'

'Isn't that a fact?' Logan drawled indolently, but his eyes gleamed with sensual awareness, and a feeling of apprehension feathered the length of Jamie's spine.

'Okay, you two, let's hike,' Jake admonished. 'There's another five miles in front of us, and I for one want to make it back to base before nightfall.'

After a while they came out of the shadows and into the sun, its glare impossible to ignore as it sank lower in the sky. Already the Rock was changing colour, deepening from bright orange to a more subdued hue. Soon it would change again, growing fractionally darker until it became light purple, then as the sun slipped beyond the horizon it would change to a deep purple, becoming almost black as the moon rose and cast a shadowy glow.

The dimension of each gulley and erosion changed with the lengthening shadows, so that the huge monolith never appeared the same for very long. As they continued, mulga gave way to more sparsely-covered soil, then in patches cleared and became dotted with spinifex. Occasionally they halted for a drink from the canvas water-bag Logan carried, and Jake frequently fell behind as he took shot after shot with his camera. About halfway he paused to re-load another film, and Jamie had to concede that he was taking no chances on any of the shots turning out.

'Tomorrow morning we climb from here,' Logan indicated, extending an arm towards the sloping rock-face. 'As you can see, we have a brisk walk from the camping area.'

A brisk walk—two and a half, possibly three, miles? Then she had to face a goodly climb up there? Jamie groaned inaudibly.

It was after eight when they reached the camping area, and she wondered wearily if she could possibly give in to tiredness and claim an early night. A long cool drink, followed by a shower, then she'd curl down into her sleeping-bag.

'Reckon you might join Jake and me in a beer?' Logan asked, slanting her a quizzical gleam as he unzipped the front flap of the tent, and she grinned appreciatively.

'I thought you'd never ask!'

'All this fresh air and sunshine,' Jake enthused, entering the tent behind them. 'These rugged conditions—makes a man feel like a pioneer. Hell, it's hot in here—but mercifully no flies,' he grinned gleefully. 'If I had to choose between one or the other, the heat would win hands down every time!'

Logan crossed to the large cooler and took out three cans of chilled beer, tossed one to each of them, then pulled the tab on his own.

'I'll set up the portable gas cooker in a few minutes. Tinned stew and bread, followed by tinned fruit?'

Jamie glanced across the space between them and inclined her head. 'Sounds fine by me.'

'I've got enough film,' Jake declared, carefully packing his camera into its case. Tomorrow I'll get some different shots while we're up top, and then when we're airborne I'll take a few more. Between them all, some must be suitable for what Barry requires.'

Logan took a long draught of beer, then eyed Jamie speculatively. 'Well, what's your opinion of the famed Rock?'

'Terrific,' she responded genuinely. 'I wouldn't have missed it for anything.'

'We'll get up before dawn, breakfast, then make an early start. It looks spectacular as the sun rises over the horizon. One is aware of the colour changes more vividly.' He drained the contents of the can, crushed it effortlessly and threw it into an empty carton. 'I'm for a shower. Jamie?'

Startled, she was temporarily lost for words, then common sense returned, and with it, memory. There were separate facilities housed in a concrete block unit less than fifty yards distant. 'You go on ahead,' she said coolly. 'I'll be along just as soon as I finish my beer.'

His eyes glinted with wicked humour, and she could have thrown the half-empty can at him very easily. He was an enigma, she mused reflectively. At times a tease, easy to talk to, then conversely a brute, cynical and almost world-weary. And adept at handling a woman in his arms, she added wryly. Undoubtedly an expert in bed. Well, she didn't aim to end up there! So far she'd managed to elude that, and it wasn't through lack of being asked. She hadn't yet met a man with whom she wanted to share sexual intimacies. Until now, a tiny voice taunted. Logan—loving him would be both heaven and hell. And while she longed to taste heaven, she had no desire to experience hell! It would be best to avoid him altogether, then she couldn't get hurt. Because he would take what he wanted, then move on. He had that certain quality, some called it machismo—an elusive sensuality meshed with animal magnetism, and combining dangerously with a superb physique. He couldn't fail to be aware of it and the effect it had, but there was nothing of the exhibitionist in his manner, and she doubted he regarded it as bearing any significance.

'Well, I've finished,' Jake declared, tossing down his empty can. 'I think I'll follow Logan's example.' He sorted through his canvas rucksack, then extracted a towel and a change of clothes. 'See you soon,' he bade with a cheeky grin as he slipped out through the tent flap, and Jamie took a generous sip of beer and almost succeeded in choking.

So much for nonchalance! Recovered, she finished the contents of the can, then crossed to her bag. There was a choice between jeans or jeans! A blue blouse, or one of multi-coloured checks. Hardly haute couture, she mused. Grabbing up a towel and a change of underwear, she selected a pair of jeans at random and decided on the blue blouse.

The shower cubicles were empty, and Jamie undressed quickly and turned on the water, luxuriating in the feel of cool water and soap against her skin. It was delicious, just out of this world, she enthused silently as she soaped herself all over, then rinsed off the suds. Careful of the need to conserve water, she hastily turned off the tap the instant she had finished, then patted her body dry, completed her toilette and quickly donned clean clothes. Mmn, now she felt almost human again, clean, and relatively cool!

As she moved towards the tent she hummed to herself, happier than she had felt in ages. Her hair hung loose about her shoulders, cascading halfway down her back in a glorious cloud of shining silk, moving with each step she took as if it had a life all its own.

She zipped open the tent-flap and stepped inside, closing it after her, then turned to find Logan and Jake sitting cross-legged on the groundsheet, a plate of steaming food before them.

Logan had changed, exchanging levis for casual trousers, and a short-sleeved cotton shirt replaced the khaki bush shirt he had worn during the day.

He looked well-groomed, refreshed and totally male.

In that instant he looked up and smiled, and Jamie felt something inside her begin to melt.

'Come and sit down,' he invited, indicating the space beside him. 'Here's your plate.'

After the tasty meal they rinsed the few plates, then Logan turned to her.

'Do you fancy joining us in a game of poker?'

Why not? She no longer felt sleepy, and she hadn't brought anything to read. 'Okay,' she acquiesced, moving over and sinking down on to the ground. 'What are the stakes?'

Jake uttered a whoop of delight as he shot her an audacious grin. "I declare the girl's a gambler! Show us the colour of your money.'

'A cent, or multiples,' Logan declared evenly, and gave a chuckle at the expression on Jake's face. 'Jamie is a working girl—she can't afford to lose too much.'

'I'm no expert,' she denied with a smile, wrinkling her nose expressively. 'But I have played the game once or twice before. Deal, Macduff,' she bade Jake, and poked out her tongue in retaliation to Logan's subdued shout of laughter.

Jamie lost by an outrageous margin, but it was fun, and she couldn't remember enjoying herself so much in a long time. It was ten o'clock when she stood gracefully to her feet hiding a wholesome yawn. 'You two can continue for as long as you like, but I'm for bed.'

Logan's eyes were frankly teasing. 'Sweet dreams, pint-size. I'll wake you in the morning.'

'That's an endearment?' Jake queried, and Logan grinned.

'Look at her—the top of her head barely reaches my shoulder.'

'I'm looking—and I like what I see.'

'Goodnight,' said Jamie, trying to hide the way her heart leapt, and with hardly a backward glance she crossed to where her sleeping-bag reposed beside her bag.

'Let's all try to get some sleep,' suggested Logan, standing to his feet, and Jake followed his example.

There was at least two feet between each of the sleeping-bags, and Jamie felt her stomach lurch crazily when Logan stretched his length down next to her. It was too hot to do anything other than use each sleeping-bag as a mattress, and she tried to ignore Logan's disturbing presence by concentrating on Jake's action of turning the small spirit lamp down until the light flickered, plunging the tent into total darkness.

Jamie regulated her breathing, consciously making it slow and even. Her heartbeat seemed to be unnecessarily loud, and she tried to think of something that would occupy her mind until she fell asleep. Idly she wriggled her toes, then carefully stretched her limbs. She closed her eyes and endeavoured to reflect over the past two years, the different people she had met and the numerous towns she had passed through on her travels. It beat counting sheep, and within a short space of time she drifted off to sleep.

'Come on, sleeping beauty!' a deep voice drawled close by, and gradually Jamie's eyes became accustomed to the gloom, and she gave a start of surprise as she glimpsed Logan crouched down on his haunches beside her.

'What are you doing here?'

His expression was impossible to discern in the semi-darkness, but his voice when he answered held laughter.

'Left alone, you'd sleep for another hour or two. There's coffee waiting for you, and beans on toast. We need to leave in ten minutes if we're to catch the dawn.' With easy grace he stood to his feet and moved out through the flap, and with a prodigious yawn Jamie scrambled upright.

Within minutes she had straightened her blouse, then she tugged a brush through her hair and wound it up on top of her head, fixing it in place with several pins. Grabbing up a towel and her toilet bag, she moved quickly towards the wash-room facilities and speedily dealt with the necessities, then she stepped hurriedly back to the tent.

Breakfast was the antithesis of a leisurely meal, and conscious of the two men's desire to leave, she ignored the beans and nibbled at her toast as she sipped the delicious hot coffee, then she collected her camera and a hat and followed Logan and Jake outside.

The first delicate tinge of light was barely visible, and they set out at a moderate pace, covering the two-mile distance to the Rock's base where access to its cairn was designated.

Jamie viewed the steep slant a trifle dubiously. A goodish climb, and not for the faint of heart, she decided. Well, she could hardly back down now!

'Jake can go first, and I'll bring up the rear,' Logan said from beside her, and she pulled a face at him.

'One to drag me up, the other to catch me if I fall,' she decided ruefully.

'A little thing like you? Light of foot, and weighing no more than thistledown? You'll fly up,' he declared sardonically, and she had to concede twenty minutes later that it hadn't been as difficult as she'd imagined. Steep, but she hadn't looked down until she reached the top.

The view was well worth it. How different everything looked when viewed from above! Two fellow-tourists walking on the ground below looked lilliputian, and she copied Jake's actions with the camera.

The descent was a little tricky in one or two places where the rock sloped sharply, and she accepted Logan's hand without question until they were almost to the ground.

Already the flies were out in droves, voraciously seeking moisture from any source available, and it was too early in the day to feel irritated by their presence.

'Well, was it worth it?'

Jamie glanced up at Logan and nodded silently. 'I wouldn't have missed it. My parents will love the photos.'

He reached out and took her camera. 'Stand over there, child, and smile. I'll record your presence here for posterity.'

The 'child' rankled somewhat. Was that all he saw her as? Too young and immature to be treated as an adult—a woman? Yet he'd kissed her—only once, it was true, but hardly in a fashion one would adopt with a child. Thinking about it made her shiver, feathering goosebumps down the length of her spine. Oh, this would never do, she decided crossly.

'Okay, I guess that's enough,' he dismissed, looking round for Jake. 'Let's head back. There's a good chance I may be able to organise a trip to the Olgas. There's a Land Rover leaving at nine, and with luck there'll be room for us.'

There was, although it was a bit crowded, and Jamie was supremely conscious of Logan sitting so close beside her for the twenty-mile drive. She sat

Harlequin Romance 1451

The Arrogant Duke
ANNE MATHER

Harlequin Romance

Beyond the Sweet Waters
ANNE HAMPSON

Harlequin Romance 884

Cap Flamingo
VIOLET WINSPEAR

Harlequin Romance

Teachers Must Learn
NERINA HILLIARD

4 FREE
Harlequin Romances

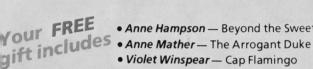

Your FREE gift includes
- *Anne Hampson* — Beyond the Sweet Waters
- *Anne Mather* — The Arrogant Duke
- *Violet Winspear* — Cap Flamingo
- *Nerina Hilliard* — Teachers Must Learn

FREE GIFT CERTIFICATE
and Subscription Reservation

Mail this card today!

Harlequin Reader Service,

Please send me my 4 Harlequin Romance novels
FREE. Also, reserve a subscription to the 6 NEW
Harlequin Romance novels published each
month. Each month I will receive 6 NEW Romance
novels at the low price of $1.25 each (Total – $7.50 a
month). There are no shipping and handling nor
any other hidden charges. I may cancel this
arrangement at any time, but even if I do, these
first 4 books are still mine to keep.

CR110

NAME _____
(PLEASE PRINT)

ADDRESS _____

CITY _____ STATE/PROV. ____ ZIP/POSTAL CODE

Take these **4** best-selling Harlequin Romance stories **FREE**

... **K** EXCITING DETAILS INSIDE

up front, and was bumped and jostled as the sturdy vehicle traversed the dusty track westward towards the group of oddly-shaped rocks visible from Ayers Rock.

A group of sandstone boulders, known to the aborigines as *Katajuta*, held less of an impact than the Rock itself, but were nonetheless of scenic interest. Rising from an arid plain, they wore stunted mulga and spinifex like a fringed skirt at their base, and there were several deep gulleys that were dangerous to the unwary.

Logan had tossed the cooler into the rear of the Land Rover, and they had a quick meal of sandwiches washed down with beer before heading back. The Cessna was due in at three, and the tent had to be dismantled and packed, and their belongings taken out to the airstrip.

Jamie took several more photos, although only a few compared to the many Jake snapped, and it seemed something of an anti-climax as they stood ready to board the plane. It had been a wonderful two days, something she would treasure for a lifetime.

Why did it always seem to take less time on the return trip? Yesterday morning it had seemed to take hours, yet now they hardly seemed airborne than they were flying over the outskirts of Alice Springs. Then she was saying goodbye to Jake as Logan dropped him off in the centre of town, and in less than five minutes he had drawn the Land Rover to a halt outside the flat.

Jamie hesitated, unsure whether to invite him in, yet oddly reluctant to say goodbye. 'Thanks for taking me,' she found herself murmuring politely. 'It was great, really, and I appreciate you including me. You didn't need to, but I'm glad you did.' Oh lord, she was making an utter mess of it! What she must say next would prove difficult, and she lifted her eyes to meet his enigmatic gaze. 'I'd like to pay my share, Logan.'

A glint of anger was quickly replaced by seeming amusement. 'You came along as my guest, Jamie,' he informed her quizzically. 'Is that so difficult to accept?'

She ran the edge of her tongue over her lower lip as she reflected, then offered quietly, 'That's very kind of you, but unless you have any objection I'd prefer to contribute something.'

'I do object,' Logan responded silkily, and her eyes widened fractionally as she gazed at him with mute appeal. His hand reached out and he touched his fingers against her lips, silencing her. 'No arguments, understand?'

Jamie felt her mouth begin to tremble and she moved towards the door. 'Thank you. I'll just get my gear.' She slipped out from the passenger seat and moved round to the rear of the vehicle to find that he was already there, reaching inside to retrieve her bag, and he handed it to her solemnly, his expression inscrutable in the early evening light. There was nothing else she could say, and she looked at him in silence, aware as never before of the overpowering virility he projected.

She almost swayed towards him, then abruptly caught hold of her wayward emotions. He didn't care, she reminded herself angrily. To him she was just a nuisance, a child, someone he'd never see again, and definitely not a woman he needed or with whom he wanted to maintain contact.

Well, this was it, the great goodbye scene—only it was nothing, just a great big empty void. Oh God, in a minute she'd begin to cry! She had to get away fast, or she'd provide him with some amusement, and that would never do! She forced a brilliant smile to her lips, then turned and walked up the path, and she didn't look back.

The flat was empty, and in the kitchen a note fluttered from its magneted anchor on the refrigerator door. Jamie removed it and slowly read the hasty scrawl explaining that Susan was out for the day and wouldn't be back until very late. For the first time in two years Jamie felt utterly alone, and lonely. The obvious thing to do was to combat it with work, and there was plenty, she determined ruefully as she cast her eyes around the flat.

Two hours later she slipped beneath the shower, and then into bed, determined to sleep in spite of the premonition that she would find it difficult to summon that somnolent state.

CHAPTER SEVEN

MONDAY passed with incredible lassitude, and Tuesday looked to follow suit. Jamie left the hotel shortly after six o'clock and walked the several blocks to the flat. With Susan on evening shift, the station wagon was left at her disposal.

The thought of preparing a meal for herself was totally lacking in appeal, and Jamie entered the kitchen feeling hot, enervated and thirsty. Dropping her bag on the table she crossed to the refrigerator and took out a can of fruit juice. There was some cheese, a few slices of ham, a tomato and some lettuce, and she nibbled disinterestedly.

Susan had brought in the washing and deposited it in a heap on the table, and Jamie moved over and began to fold it tidily. Ten minutes later she was beneath the shower.

Just as she was about to step into clean underwear there was a knock at the door, and with a start she flung on a silky wrap and flew out to answer the repeated summons.

Caution insisted she determine just who was standing on the other side of the door, and she asked the necessary question a trifle apprehensively.

There was silence for a brief second, then a familiar voice drawled, 'Friend, not foe, Jamie. Open up!'

Logan! Slowly she opened the door, schooling her features to resemble politeness instead of the intense joy his presence aroused. 'Hello,' she greeted quietly.

He stood leaning against the door-jamb, looking

indomitable in dark trousers and a dark shirt unbuttoned almost to the waist. His smile was quizzical and faintly teasing. 'Aren't you going to ask
me in?'

'I've just got out from the shower—I'm not even
dressed,' she faltered, annoyed with the way her
heart was pounding.

'Then go and get changed,' Logan directed
lazily. 'I'm taking you out to dinner.'

Oh, he was so sure of himself—of *her*. 'Are
you?' she queried with some attempt at *savoir faire*,
and was further enraged when he began to laugh.
'It's usual to ask a girl first,' she flung with marked
asperity, standing aside so that he could enter.

With a laugh he caught her close and kissed her
—slowly and with evident enjoyment. 'There—
now will you come?'

He was impossible! But the temptation was too
great, and she wrinkled her nose at him, her eyes
sparkling with mischief. 'Oh, very well. I'll be
five minutes—maybe a few more.'

In her room she went straight to her wardrobe.
He hadn't said where he was taking her, but she
selected a dress she had bought in Sydney more
than a year ago. Of deep emerald green, it was of
soft silk crêpe de chine, cunningly cut with a
draped bodice that was more daring than she
usually wore, and a skirt that swirled with every
movement she made. High-heeled sandals completed the outfit, and she used a minimum of make-
up, preferring a natural look, and highlighted her
eyes with mascara and eyeshadow. She stroked a
brush through her hair, leaving it loose, then she
picked up an evening purse and emerged into the
lounge.

Logan's admiring glance sent delicious tingles
soaring through her veins, and she felt as if she

were treading on air as she followed him out to the Land Rover.

'I thought we'd visit the Steakhouse,' Logan declared as he set the heavy vehicle in motion. 'If you'd prefer somewhere else, don't hesitate to say so.'

'That sounds fine,' she agreed, uncaring where they went, knowing that she probably wouldn't taste a thing anyway.

The restaurant was well patronised, but a table was found for them and Jamie allowed Logan to order for her.

'What will you do now the compaction unit has completed its job?' she asked, and Logan smiled.

'I'm due in Adelaide at the beginning of next week. There's some business I must attend to there, then I'll return to Melbourne.'

'Oh.' Disappointment was just barely held at bay. 'Do you live in Melbourne?' She looked down at her plate and became intent on slicing the knife through her steak, and missed the gleam of amusement in his eyes.

'Most of the time,' he replied easily. 'I travel around a lot.'

'Road construction?'

'Mostly.' His response was noncommittal, and Jamie endeavoured to steer the conversation into different channels.

'Do you play any sport?' A ridiculous question to ask a man so obviously at the peak of physical vitality—one had only to look at him!

His eyes shone with hidden laughter. 'Relax, Jamie. You don't have to entertain me. Eat,' he bade kindly.

Why did she have to feel so immature and unsure of herself whenever she was with him? Usually she could command a witty conversation and be an amusing companion, but with Logan she was reduced to a tongue-tied schoolgirl on her first date.

It was after nine when they left the steak restaurant, and at Logan's suggestion they strolled towards the nearest hotel with the intention of drinking a glass or two of beer.

The lounge was crowded, but they managed to find a small table in the beer garden, and Jamie took a seat while Logan went to the bar and ordered their drinks.

When he returned she sipped the icy liquid pensively, letting her eyes slide surreptitiously over his arresting features.

Fool, she chastised herself mentally—he's out of your reach, forget him. But how could she—when the memory of his kiss evoked a warmth in her lower limbs and set her pulse racing crazily? Such a sensuously-moulded mouth, whose lips could wreak havoc to her awakening senses. Her eyes lingered there, then lifted and were quickly averted as she met his steadfast gaze.

'Let's go.'

It was a statement of intention, not a suggestion, and in silence she followed him outside.

Within five minutes the Land Rover had drawn to a halt outside the flat, and she burst into hesitant speech.

'Would you like to come in?' Nervousness lowered her voice to an indistinct murmur.

'Why not?' Logan slipped the catch and slid out from behind the wheel, and she hurriedly vacated the vehicle.

The flat was empty, for Susan was working until ten, and had indicated earlier that she was going out on a date straight afterwards and wouldn't be home until late.

'Would you like coffee?' Jamie queried. 'Or there's beer in the refrigerator if you'd prefer it.'

Carefully Logan shut the door, then he reached out and drew her steadily towards him. 'You talk too much,' he admonished quietly, and she gasped out loud.

'Logan——'

'Shh!' he ordered, pulling her into his arms, and there was little she could do to escape the descending mouth as he kissed her.

His lips were hard and warm, and after a few seconds she gave up trying to resist him, her lips parting beneath his as he insistently probed them apart, beginning a sensual onslaught that totally obliterated everything else. Of their own volition her arms crept up and wound themselves around his neck, and if it were possible he caught her even closer against him, making her shockingly aware of his needs.

His lips trailed a provocative path down her throat, then teased the delicate hollows at its base before moving slowly up to nuzzle an earlobe. Hands caressed her back, then moved tantalisingly over each collar-bone, sliding the straps of her dress down over each shoulder.

As his fingers sought a creamy breast her sanity returned, and she surfaced from the overwhelming sensual tide of emotion. 'No,' she protested breathlessly, her eyes large dark pools as she gazed up at him. 'Logan—stop it!' She began to struggle in earnest, suddenly afraid of what she had invited.

'Stop?' he queried softly, his eyes brilliant with passion. 'Jamie, my sweet, I've hardly begun,' he teased, close to her mouth.

'Logan, I mean it,' she insisted shakily, twisting her head to one side. 'Please let me go.' She stood very still, her mouth trembling, its softness faintly bruised.

Silently he put her at arms' length, and she lifted a shaky hand to push a length of her hair back behind her ear.

'You want me,' he stated softly. 'Why?'

A delicate tinge of pink crept over her cheeks, and she was powerless to stop the tears that welled up behind her eyes. It seemed as if someone had taken control of her voice, for she wasn't capable of uttering a word. The silence between them seemed interminable, and at last she offered huskily, 'I'm sorry, I don't——' she faltered, then said more clearly, 'I won't go to bed with you, Logan. If—if I gave you the impression that I—would, I'm sorry.'

His arms dropped away and he stood in silence, his expression guarded, and something—some indefinable niggle worried her brain, making her raise her head to look at him more closely. He didn't appear devastated by her refusal, nor was he attempting to cajole her into changing her mind.

'You—you were testing me, weren't you?' she accused, trembling with indignation, and when he failed to deny it she stepped back a pace and turned away. 'Get out of here, Logan,' she said quietly. 'I never want to see you again.'

'Jamie——'

'Perhaps I should run a test on you!' she uttered wrathfully. 'I don't know who you are—your surname—— Anything! You—you just turn up, offer me a trip to Ayers Rock, then you—you leave. Tonight you arrive on my doorstep and—and coldbloodedly——' Words failed her, and she began walking towards her bedroom intent only on getting away from him.

'Jamie.'

She halted, then turned round, uncaring of the tears slowly trickling down her cheeks. 'I hate you!' she declared.

His gaze was steady. 'I could have used words, assembling them into any of the hackneyed phrases you wanted to hear.'

'What stopped you?' Jamie asked, then offered pityingly, 'I feel sorry for you, Logan. Now, will you please go.'

He gazed across the room at her for what seemed an age, then silently he turned and walked out the door, closing it quietly behind him. If he had slammed it, she would have felt better, but the silent action bothered her more than she cared to admit.

For a long time she stood where she was, unable to move. In spite of the heat she felt cold, and her heart felt heavy. She wanted to cry, but she was too numb.

To forget Logan, Jamie threw herself into work, spending her free time effecting a clean-up of the flat, and during her hours behind the bar she volunteered for chores that were beyond her normal duties. She began to look forward to the times when the bar was crammed with customers, for then she was too busy to think.

By Friday she was beginning to feel like an automaton, even her smile seemed mechanical, and Susan was beginning to get suspicious. Somehow Jamie was able to steer clear of too many questions by pleading the onset of a cold, although she doubted it fooled Susan. Soon she would be obliged to tell her, and raking over the ashes wasn't something she looked forward to at all.

There was a party on this evening, but she couldn't face being among a crowd. For about the fifth time she refused Susan's invitation to come, and she slipped into the passenger seat of the station wagon with the weariness of someone twice her age.

'Why not come, Jamie? It will do you good,' Susan began persuasively, shooting her friend an anxious glance.

'The only thing that will do me good is a shower followed by bed,' Jamie declared wearily. 'Look, I'm all right—just tired, that's all. You go on and enjoy yourself.'

'Something's bothering you, and I have a pretty good idea what it is,' the other girl declared, and Jamie lifted a hand in a gesture of defeat.

'Don't bother turning into the driveway,' she instructed. 'Just pull over to the curb.' She sat up in the seat, her hand on the door-clasp. 'I'll see you in the morning.' She slipped out and closed the door behind her, then waved as the station wagon moved forward.

Dear Lord, she felt tired! It had been quite a week, one way and another. She began walking up the path, shadows masking the front porch until she almost collided with him.

'Oh!' She stopped dead in her tracks, fear uppermost, then recognition brought anger. 'What are you doing here?'

'Can we go inside?' Logan countered evenly, and she shook her head.

'What for? I have nothing to say to you.' She moved past him and pushed the key into the lock, ignoring him, but as she opened the door he moved so quickly that he was inside before she could stop him.

'Go away!' Fury darkened her eyes, making

them almost black, and unconsciously her fingers clenched until her nails dug painfully into each palm.

He regarded her silently, his expression enigmatic, then slowly he withdrew a piece of paper and held it out. 'You're due in Adelaide in a few weeks,' he began imperturbably. 'If you'll contact me when you arrive, I'll see to it there's a job for you. Susan, too.'

'I don't need your help, Logan.'

'Jobs aren't that easy to find. It may take a few weeks—it's expensive trying to set up accommodation, and if you have to wait too long for a job ...' he let his voice trail off, then he leaned forward and pressed the paper into her hand.

'Is that it?' Jamie asked stiffly. 'Will you go now?'

'Not quite.' His head bent low as his hands grasped hold of her shoulders, and he gently touched his lips against the edge of her mouth.

She stood perfectly still, forcing herself to remain passive as he kissed her, then she was free and he was gone.

Her knees felt as if they would collapse, and she hastily crossed to the nearest chair. Oh God, why did he have to come back? she groaned. It wasn't fair. Slowly she unfolded the sheet of paper, scanning it for something other than the group of numbers written there, but there was nothing—no name or address, just a telephone number.

During the following weeks Jamie determinedly put Logan out of her mind, and as the time drew near for them to leave Alice Springs she began to look forward to the train journey down to Port Pirie. Extensive enquiries had revealed that the road between Alice Springs and Port Pirie was very rough, and on advice from the automobile club they had decided to freight the station wagon down and travel as passengers. Everything was arranged for them to depart the first week in March, and they worked right up until the last day. There was a weekly rail service between Alice Springs and Port Pirie, and the train departed each Wednesday evening, taking almost three days to reach its destination in South Australia.

The station wagon had to be consigned to the railway station early in the morning, and they deposited their luggage at the same time, then spent the day visiting places of interest around the main township until they were due to board the train.

Travelling at night was a novel experience, and their berth was comfortable and functional. For the remainder of the first day the scenery outside the train window was an unchanging pattern of arid land unbroken except for clumps of spinifex, but when they rose on Friday morning the terrain showed a subtle change. Green it wasn't, as it was the end of the summer, but there were trees and a variety of scrub that made a pleasant change from the mulga and spinifex abounding for several hundred square miles adjacent to the border between Northern Territory and South Australia.

The train was late arriving at Port Pirie, and it was almost six o'clock on Friday evening before they disembarked and a further hour before they were able to ascertain that the station wagon wouldn't be offloaded until the following morning.

Overnight accommodation wasn't difficult to find, for they were able to bed down at a youth hostel, and it was a relief to discover the station wagon parked waiting for them to collect early on Saturday morning. It was almost a two-hour drive through to Adelaide and they arrived shortly before midday.

Their first priority was to buy a newspaper, and they pored over the number of flats available, rang several, then armed with a map they endeavoured to find suitable accommodation.

By the end of the day they had moved into a small functional flat in the suburb of Henley. They could have chosen something closer to the city, but the nearby beach swayed them considerably in its favour. Sunday was spent settling in, and on Monday they were on the doorstep of the local shop for a copy of the daily newspaper. For now they must find work, preferably office work if they could get it.

Armed with a list of telephone numbers, they began, but because of the general economic situation it wasn't as easy as they had hoped, and as the days went by with each interview bringing the usual 'we'll contact you', they became dispirited. The main stumbling block was that they were New Zealanders, and although they assured prospective employers that they intended to remain in the city for a minimum of six months, they were met with caution and a certain disbelief.

Although they had allowed for a fortnight without any money coming in, it was becoming imperative they find work soon.

Jamie thought of the slip of paper Logan had given her, but pride refused to allow her to contact him. If she was forced to, she would telephone him as a last resort.

As it turned out, they did each secure a position, although it was hardly glamorous—Susan was helping in the kitchen of a large hospital, and Jamie, who had done a waitressing stint for a few months in Surfer's Paradise, went to work as a waitress in an exclusive city restaurant. Transport was a slight problem because of their diverse working hours, so it was decided that as Susan had an early morning start she would take the station wagon, then when she finished work she would drive it into the city, leaving it for Jamie's use at night, then catch the bus back to the flat.

Jamie began work at eleven-thirty to cover the lunch-hour trade, went off at two-thirty, then reported again at five and finished at eleven. The worst part was filling in the two and a half hours in the afternoon, for it was hardly worth going back to the flat, although on one or two occasions she did, and she explored the city, visiting a museum, cathedrals and churches of which there were several, or frequented the library. Sunday and Monday nights were her only evenings off, but after the first few weeks she grew accustomed to her working hours and the routine.

On Wednesday evening of the third week there was nothing to give Jamie warning that anything untoward would occur, but it did, in the shape of Logan putting in an appearance.

His presence at one of her tables gave her an unwanted jolt, and his companion was gorgeous —a statuesque blonde with wealthy sophistication stamped all over her elegantly attired body.

For a moment she considered pleading illness, but disregarded the temptation. There was nothing else for it but to go over there and take the order.

Wearing a fixed smile she moved forward, greeted them politely, and handed each a menu.

Logan's surprise wasn't visible, although he greeted her by name, thus causing a ripple of speculation from his companion, who regarded Jamie thoughtfully for all of twenty seconds.

He looked totally different from the man she had

known almost two months previously and about as far removed from an earthmoving driver as it was possible to imagine. His dark grey suit was impeccably tailored and expensive, and he bore the air of a city executive.

'I think I'll have mushrooms as an entree, followed by chicken Maryland, darling,' the blonde declared in a bored voice. 'And a green salad.'

Logan deliberated, then looked up to consider Jamie thoughtfully. 'What would you suggest, Jamie?'

Oh, he was being impossible! she decided crossly. 'If you like shellfish, the lobster thermidor is excellent, or the prawns,' she intimated civilly. 'Otherwise duck à l'orange, or perhaps the steak Diane.'

'Lobster, I think,' he determined. 'No entree, but like Sacha I'll have a green salad.'

Sacha! It was exotic and foreign, and suited its bearer admirably. 'Thank you, sir,' Jamie responded formally. 'The wine steward will be along in a minute to take your order.'

After that Jamie was supremely conscious of them, despite the fact that the restaurant was filled to capacity and she was extremely busy.

Perforce she had to serve them each course, and lastly coffee, and on each occasion she was aware of Logan's interested gaze. It was a miracle that she didn't drop a plate or spill anything!

Eventually they left, but when she went to clear their table she found a ten-dollar note tucked beneath the coffee pot. How dared he! she raged silently. Tipping wasn't the normal practice, although some customers left a note of small denomination as an expression of pleasure for the service given, but ten dollars was practically unheard of. Slowly she folded it and placed it in her pocket.

When—*if* she saw him again, she would return it.

The following morning she reported for work, and after changing into the long batik skirt and a short-sleeved black knit top that comprised her uniform, she smoothed her hair and walked through into the main restaurant to check the tables. The tablecloths were all neatly draped over each table, but there was still the cutlery to set, and she deftly completed her section before checking through the menu. Within minutes the main outside door would be unlocked and the first of the day's patrons would enter.

Jamie stood to one side, ready, while the manager moved towards the entrance, and then in a steady flow patrons filtered inside requiring attention.

It was after midday when she turned and saw that another of her tables had just become occupied, and her stomach lurched crazily when she recognised the occupant. Logan—again!

She crossed to his side and solemnly handed him a menu, the smile on her lips nowhere near reaching her eyes.

'If you'd care to order,' she suggested quietly. 'Otherwise I'll return in a few minutes.'

'The gazpacho, Jamie,' he said blandly. 'Followed by a salad—ham, I think.'

She inclined her head and retreated, concentrating her attention on the other tables, oddly loath to serve the strangely enigmatic man openly watching her every move.

As she placed the soup on the table before him, he looked across and smiled.

'You're free for a few hours this afternoon. Will you allow me to show you something of the city?'

'I don't think so—thank you,' she replied evenly, and he shook his head slightly.

'Then perhaps you'll meet me for coffee after you finish up here tonight?'

'That's not possible,' she refused politely, and he shot her a quizzical glance.

'Jamie, I'd like to take you out. If necessary, I'll have lunch here every day until you accept dinner as well.'

'You're mad,' she stated flatly, and turning away she walked to the kitchen to collect the course she was to serve to table three.

Before long she had to take Logan's salad, and she approached his table with a feeling of trepidation.

'I have something of yours I wish to return,' she said firmly, withdrawing the folded ten-dollar note. 'It's not customary to tip, and I certainly can't accept this.' She placed it beside his plate, feeling faintly afraid. Somehow the action seemed to invite retribution, yet there wasn't much she could do about it. It wasn't the money, it was the principle of the thing.

Calmly he accepted it, taking the note between thumb and forefinger he neatly folded it several times, then raised his hand and pushed it firmly between the opening of her top so that it nestled between the softness of her breasts.

Angrily Jamie withdrew it and flung it down on the table. 'I don't *want* your money!' she hissed furiously. 'And you can't force me to accept it!' Turning, she walked away.

Logan's silence throughout the remainder of the meal was disquieting, and she heaved a sigh of relief when she saw him leave. Perhaps he'd got the messages at last, and he wouldn't bother her any more.

At exactly two-thirty Jamie slipped out the side entrance and stepped briskly towards the main street. She had changed into a dress of bright cotton print that highlighted her deep brown hair and accentuated her slim petite figure. Light sandals on her feet added three inches to her height, and it felt good to be out in the fresh air with a few hours to spare before she had to return. She had no plans, but there were so many parks it would be nice to wander through one or two and admire the flowers and shrubs.

She turned on to the main street and came to an abrupt halt, for standing beside a parked car was Logan, his arms crossed and expression of studied patience creasing his rugged countenance.

Jamie made to walk past, but he reached out a hand and grasped her arm.

'Get in, Jamie.'

The look she flung him had no effect, and she almost stamped her foot from sheer rage. 'No! And if you don't leave me alone,' she threatened, 'I'll summon a policeman and report you for harrassment.'

'Do that,' Logan shrugged negligibly. 'I'll kiss you until you're giddy right in front of his nose, then explain that you're upset over a silly lovers' tiff.'

'You wouldn't dare!'

'Try me,' he declared softly, dangerously. 'Now, will you get in?'

'Why should I?'

'I'd rather argue with you in the relative privacy of my car. However, if you want to fight here in open view of everyone passing by, then so be it.'

'I don't wan't to argue,' she cried, sorely tried. 'I don't even want to *talk* to you!'

'Why are you so upset?' he pursued quietly. 'I refuse to believe I was the first man who tried to get you into bed. It was a natural action—we both wanted it.'

'You may accept sex as the normal end to a date, but I don't. It wasn't that that upset me,' she paused to draw breath. 'It was the manner in which you did it.'

'And if I promise not to lay a hand on you, will you come out with me?'

Jamie looked at him carefully. 'Why me, Logan? You obviously don't lack for feminine company.'

'No,' he agreed. 'However, I seem to be interested in a five-foot-two-inch Kiwi brunette.'

'You're mad,' she said unsteadily, and saw his lips twist into a grim smile.

'It is madness. I've never chased after a woman in my life. Now, will you please get into this car? I'll drive you on to the Mount Lofty Ranges. It's only twenty-five minutes from here, and the view is superb.'

Indecision creased her brow, then she capitulated. 'Can you get me back by five?'

He gave a brief affirmative, and feeling as if she were about to enter through a door from which there could be no escape Jamie moved round the rear of the vehicle and slipped into the passenger seat.

The car eased forward into the stream of traffic, and for the entire twenty-five minutes Logan didn't utter so much as a word.

As he had promised, the view was incredible, and she wished she had her camera so that she could record it. The city lay spread before them, the numerous parks providing a checkerboard panorama amidst the conglomerate of concrete buildings of varying height and architecture. Neat wide streets were tree-lined, and in the suburbs a sprinkling of multi-coloured rooftops added bright splashes of colour that were visually pleasing. At night it would be a positive fairyland with its tracery of street-lights and flashing neons.

'It's beautiful,' Jamie breathed softly, and Logan nodded, his eyes not on the view.

'Yes. What time do you finish tonight? I'll take you on to a nightclub.'

She looked up at him, then shook her head. 'I can't, not tonight.'

'Can't, or won't?'

'Susan and I have an arrangement about transport. Besides,' Jamie explained, 'I didn't bring anything suitable to wear to a nightclub.'

He regarded her steadily. 'You look fine to me.'

'You can't be serious,' she laughed jokingly.

'Tomorrow bring something suitable with you. And after lunch I'll take you to Belair recreation centre and Old Government House.'

'Don't you have to work?'

His smile was reflective and faintly teasing. 'I assure you my working hours are flexible.'

'In that case, yes, I'd like to come.'

Logan indicated the Botanic Gardens. 'Shall we wander through? By then it will be time to get back.'

They walked side by side, he tolerant when she paused to admire a particular flower or shrub, and it was almost thirty minutes before they stopped beside the car again.

'It's truly a garden city,' Jamie mused, glancing back. 'My mother would love it here. She treats each of her plants like humans,' she told him with a sparkling laugh. 'Talks to them and nurtures them as if they were children. And rarely does a weed see the light of day!'

'I look forward to meeting her.'

What did he mean by that, for heaven's sake? She didn't dare think about it. Her heart began to race, making her suddenly breathless, and to cover her agitation she opened the car door and slipped into the passenger seat.

When Logan pulled up to the curb outside the restaurant entrance he leaned across and opened her door, his arm brushing hers, and the contact made her catch her breath.

'I'll be here at two-thirty tomorrow. Until then,' he said quietly, and Jamie murmured something indistinct and hastily scrambled out to stand on the pavement, watching as he slid the car out into the traffic.

CHAPTER EIGHT

'YOU appear to have an admirer,' Georges, the wine steward, murmured as he paused near the entrance to the restaurant kitchen. 'Dinner Wednesday night, then lunch yesterday, and lunch again today. You intend going out with him?'

'I met him in Alice Springs several weeks ago,' Jamie said quietly, and his face brightened with comprehension.

'Ah, he followed you here.'

'No,' she disclaimed. 'It was just a coincidence.'

'Be careful of him—he has the look of a man who has tasted everything sweet that life has to offer. Make sure you won't be discarded.'

'He's just a friend—nothing more.'

His black brows quirked in silent disbelief. 'A woman could not be merely a *friend* to a man such as he. Watch your step, *mon amie*, hmm?'

'He doesn't have my heart,' Jamie asserted, and he shook his head.

'Not yet, perhaps. But he will.'

'Only if I allow it.'

His mocking silence openly derided her swift avowal. 'I have observed,' he shrugged eloquently. 'The chemistry, it is there between you.'

Jamie sent him a swift look beneath her lashes. 'One think I know for sure—I can't stand here talking all day. Two of my tables have just become occupied.'

Just why Logan was pursuing her had caused her to spend a restless night, and she had woken early in the morning still none the wiser. Part of her wanted to live each day as it came, with no thought of tomorrow, but an innate sense of moral inhibition placed a restraint that could not be ignored.

At two-thirty she swiftly changed from her uniform into a light sun-frock, freshened her make-up and caught up her bag and sunglasses, then made her way on to the main street.

Logan's car was parked in the identical place it had occupied the day before, and as Jamie drew close she offered him a smile that brought forth a lazy sloping grin.

'Hi,' she greeted, and he responded,

'Hi, yourself. You look cool and fresh, and good enough to eat.'

Don't say things like that, she wanted to cry out. Instead, she laughed and sent him a mischievous smile. 'Remarks like that could turn a girl's head.' She considered him thoughtfully. 'You don't look too bad, either. A whole world apart from the man I met driving a grading machine out in the middle of nowhere,' she teased, and he opened the car door with a mocking flourish.

'I refuse to bandy words with you in this heat. Get in, Jamie. Today, Belair awaits us.'

The car sped swiftly out from the city, and the next few hours were over all too soon. As they were wandering through Old Government House, Logan caught hold of her hand and didn't relinquish it until they returned to the car. Gone was the mockery that had been evident at the road-camp and at Ayers Rock, and Jamie felt his warmth tug at her heartstrings.

It was an idyllic few hours and she was genuinely sorry when he dropped her off outside the restaurant bare minutes before she was due to report for work, although his teasing 'see you at eleven' sang in her ears and carried her on a cloud through the ensuing six hours.

Reposing on a hanger and protected by thin plastic was a gown she had purchased in Brisbane several months previously, a slim-fitting, eye-catching design in cream voile that accentuated her dark hair and clear suntanned skin. Slim-heeled sandals and an evening bag completed the outfit, and she took extra time to apply fresh make-up and stroked a brush through her hair until it gleamed and shone like silk.

Logan's silence left her feeling hauntingly vulnerable and unsure her choice had been the right one, until he caught hold of her hand and carried it to his lips. The expressive gleam in those brilliant blue eyes sent the butterflies in her stomach fluttering madly, and her whole body began to glow.

The nightclub was situated only a few blocks away, and was exclusive, Jamie realised as they entered the impressive foyer. Logan was an amicable host, urbane and faintly enigmatic, and it wasn't until she had disposed of the contents of one glass of wine and sipped almost half another that she began to relax.

'Would you like to dance?'

She considered the question carefully. More than anything she wanted to be held close in his arms, but there was definite danger in doing so. The memory of what had happened in Alice Springs was still vivid in her mind, and she had no desire to encourage a repeat performance.

'Do you need so much time to think about it?' he quizzed gently, and she smiled a slow sweet smile, her mind made up.

'Nothing energetic,' she warned. 'I think I've had too much wine. I feel as if I'm floating!'

Logan's eyes gleamed with silent laughter as he

took her hand and led her on to the floor and into his arms. 'Then you'd better not drink any more. I don't want to have to carry you home and put you to bed.'

'I wouldn't let you,' Jamie said solemnly, a strange curling sensation beginning in the pit of her stomach as his arms tightened fractionally, and she could have sworn his lips touched the top of her head in a fleeting caress.

They drifted slowly around the fringe of the dance floor, and she could have remained in his arms for ever. It felt so right she almost cried at the strength of emotion that washed over her like a tide, and when Logan gently broke away she felt bereft, as if she had been torn in two. Did he feel the same, she wondered in a state of bemusement, or was it only one-sided? Too late now to think of heartache, for her soul was entwined with his as surely as if there were visible ties binding them together. If he was only playing with her, she'd wither and die.

'Logan, darling—I've given up waiting for you to call me!'

Jamie turned slowly to meet Sacha's flashing smile, and almost gasped out loud at the exotic beauty of the other girl's features. Oh God, how could she hope to compete with such perfection?

'Sacha, Nick,' Logan greeted blandly, his strong features expressing politeness and a certain warmth, and turning slightly he wound an arm about Jamie's waist. 'Sacha Andreas, her brother Nick—Jamie Prentiss.'

Jamie murmured a greeting, then lapsed into silence as Sacha caught hold of Logan's arm with elegantly-manicured hands that looked as if they'd never done a day's work.

'Oh—the charming little waitress,' she said in a disinterested voice. 'Shall we make it a foursome, darling? Nick and I were bored sitting at home without dates, so we decided to join forces and visit a few of our favourite haunts.'

Oh, she was so clever, Jamie surmised, feeling suddenly defenceless in company with the other girl's impeccable sophistication, for within minutes of being seated at their table Sacha had skilfully manoeuvred her chair close to Logan, devoting her entire attention to him and leaving Jamie conspicuously alone with Nick.

'Shall we dance?' Nick suggested in a droll voice. 'My dear sister seems to have monopolised Logan.'

Jamie was about to refuse, then she changed her mind and accepted, standing to her feet and moving towards the dance floor without more than a polite smile in Logan's direction.

Nick held her close, much too close for her liking, and she endeavoured to move away without much success.

'Are you Logan's exclusive property?'

'Does he usually confine himself to one woman?' she parried smoothly, and a knife twisted inside her as Nick uttered a laugh full of cynical scepticism.

'Sacha would like to think so, but no, I'm afraid our dear Logan plays the field.'

'You don't like him,' Jamie declared, and her companion gave a wry grimace.

'I wouldn't want him as an enemy. He wields too much power for me to want to be on the wrong side of him.'

It would have been simple to question that statement, but she didn't, and they completed the dance in silence and when the music stopped momentarily Nick led her back to the table.

As Jamie sank down into her chair she was conscious of the brief enigmatic glance Logan swept her, and it took all her courage to answer it with an

engaging smile. Then she turned her attention to
the contents of her glass, and drank the wine rather
more quickly than was wise, for she soon became
aware of its effects.

'Another, Jamie?'

She swung her head towards Nick and offered
him a brilliant smile. 'Why not?' Suddenly she felt
daring, for the alcohol was giving her a false sense
of confidence she badly needed. She didn't bother
looking at Logan, and when her glass was refilled
she picked it up and sipped the clear German
wine with a hint of defiance.

When Nick asked her to dance again she readily
accepted, and concentrated on following his intri-
cate steps to flamboyant disco music. He was an
exhibitionist, and after a while she simply stood
aside and let him continue on his own. He didn't
need a partner, he was a show all by himself.

When the music finished there was a sound of
applause which Jamie joined in, and they returned
to the table laughing over something she hadn't
the slightest conception had initiated laughter.

'I think we'd better leave,' Logan declared only
seconds after she had taken her seat, and she cast
him a deliberately enquiring glance.

'Oh, darling,' Sacha pouted prettily, placing her
hand on his jacketed forearm. 'Must you? Nick and
I plan on staying for ages. It's not late.'

But he was already on his feet and his hand
grasped hold of Jamie's arm, applying just enough
pressure to warn her not to resist. 'Another time,
perhaps,' he refused cordially, and inclining his
head towards Nick he bade them goodnight.

'Stay with your friends—I shan't mind,' Jamie
protested as he led her towards the main entrance,
but the look he cast her was grim.

'And have Nick fill your glass every ten minutes?

Nothing would give me less satisfaction,' he returned brusquely.

'He doesn't like you, either,' she broke into teasing laughter, then spoilt the effect by hiccuping. 'Oh dear,' she murmured remorsefully.

'Little girls who can't hold their liquor shouldn't drink,' Logan said hardily.

'You're angry,' she vouchsafed contritely, and he slanted her a compelling look, then sighed.

'No. I'm trying hard to decide whether I'm going to shake you or kiss you. What I should do is take you across my knee and render a hurtful spanking.'

She turned wide guileless eyes up to search his. 'I'm quite sober—well, almost,' she qualified soulfully. 'I've never been drunk in my life.'

'It wasn't the amount of wine you've consumed that I was referring to,' he maintained obliquely as he led the way to the car.

'Sacha,' Jamie mused with false interest as he switched on the ignition and engaged the gears. 'Such an unusual name. And her surname, it sounds foreign.'

'Greek,' Logan stated sardonically as he slid out into the traffic. 'She's twenty-six, single, and runs a fashion boutique. Nick is thirty, likewise single, and endeavours to help in his father's business. Anything else you want to know?'

'I don't like you when you're being sarcastic.'

'For a little girl, you sure talk a hell of a lot,' he rejoined brusquely, and she edged far back in her seat, as far away from him as possible.

'In that case, I shan't bother saying another word,' she retaliated.

'That would be advisable.'

For the remainder of the drive home Jamie sat in total silence, her eyes closed against the beginings of a headache, the effects of the wine, and sheer tiredness.

Through a hazy mist she was aware of the car's lack of motion, and when the door beside her opened she sat up and tried to swing her legs down on to the ground, emerging stumbling and attempting to regain her balance.

'Oh, for heaven's sake!' Logan swore savagely, and scooping her into his arms he carried her to the flat, extracted her keys, unlocked the door, then continued through the small lounge into the hallway. 'Which is your room?'

Jamie waved an arm over the top of his shoulder. 'Left three feet, then put me down. From there I can manage by myself.' She was sure of it, but the instant her feet touched the floor she collapsed in an elegant heap and would have fallen had Logan not caught hold of her.

What happened after that she had no recollection, except that when she woke next morning she was in bed minus most of her clothes—and nursing a gigantic headache.

Oh Lord, she groaned out loud as she emerged into a sitting position. Her head didn't belong to her at all, and her stomach had reservations also. Coffee, she needed a cup of hot black sweetened coffee, and possibly a slice of dry toast. The thought of eating breakfast was enough to make her forget food for a lifetime! A glance at her watch revealed it to be after ten, and she uttered another groan. Thirty-five minutes in which to shower, dress, drink some coffee and get to the bus stop. If only she could fall back into bed!

Then she glanced down and saw that she was wearing only her bra and pants, and events of the previous evening came flooding back in glorious Technicolor. Logan! Had he——? No, it wasn't possible that he'd spent some time in her bed. If he had, she'd feel—different. Oh, why couldn't she *remember*?

All the way into the city she puzzled how she could ever face him again, then pulled herself up with a grimace of derision. After last night he probably wouldn't want to see her, and she could hardly blame him.

Even Georges commented on her paleness and the dark circles beneath her eyes, and offered his own remedy.

'A raw tomato, pepper and salt, *mon amie*,' he declared firmly. 'Followed by a glass of water. It was quite a night, hmm?'

'Some little gremlin has entered my brain and is banging away with twin sledge-hammers,' she winced. 'I hope this works. I don't even like tomatoes,' she wailed in distaste.

'Here is the water, and when you have finished it, you will take two Disprin. Within ten minutes I guarantee you will feel human again. Trust me,' he urged with a twinkle of humour that went unnoticed as Jamie drained the glass he held out.

Logan didn't put in an appearance during the luncheon hours, not that Jamie expected him to, and she emerged out on to the main street shortly after two-thirty to find another car parked against the curb and no sign of Logan.

To fill in time before she was due to return to the restaurant she wandered into one of the large department stores, then idly browsed through several boutiques before crossing to the library where she wrote a short letter to her parents.

The evening trade was brisk, as it was Saturday night, and it was almost nine o'clock when she saw Logan enter the foyer. He didn't sit at one of her tables, although on reflection it wasn't possible as they were all occupied, and she was startlingly aware of his presence to such a degree that she found it difficult to concentrate, and had to ask more than once for a patron to repeat an order.

By the time she finished at eleven she was a mess, both physically and mentally, and she swiftly changed out of her uniform, donned the clothes she had worn in to work, then not even bothering to check her make-up she slipped out the side door with the intention of hailing a taxi.

She hadn't walked more than a dozen steps when she heard someone call her name, and she slowed to a halt and turned to see Logan's tall frame moving quickly towards her.

As she drew close she began to shake with nervous reaction, and had to force herself to greet him coolly.

'I'll take you home.'

'I was going to get a taxi,' she informed him indistinctly, and he smiled grimly.

'My car is parked just around the block. Let's go.'

'Are you always so domineering?'

'Only when I have to be.'

'I thought you'd be with Sacha tonight,' she began waspishly, and could have bitten her tongue. What was wrong with her? She was behaving like a shrew.

'Jamie,' he warned dangerously, but she couldn't stop.

'What time did you leave the flat last night, Logan?'

There was silence for several seconds, and when he spoke his voice sent chills scudding down her spine.

'If by that remark you mean did I seduce you, then I can assure that I didn't. Taking advantage of a sleeping, defenceless *child* isn't one of my vices. And if I *had* spent the night with you,' he continued with brutal honesty, 'I would still have been there when you woke this morning. I don't take my pleasure like a thief in the night,' he added ruthlessly, pausing beside the car. 'Get in, Jamie.'

'I can get a taxi,' she insisted stoically, and he gave an expressive sigh that suggested great forbearance.

'God help me,' he threatened softly, 'if you don't get into the car of your own accord, then I won't be answerable for the consequences.'

Without a word she did as she was told, and for the following fifteen minutes she sat in silence, unable to utter so much as a word. The instant the car came to a halt outside the flat she placed a hand on the clasp to open the door, only to have him reach across to prevent her escape.

'Let me out, Logan,' she demanded stormily.

'So much anger, Jamie,' he taunted quietly.

'Why are you playing games with me? Am I a challenge, or something?' she cried. 'Why *me*, Logan? When there's someone like Sacha waiting, willing and eager. She's beautiful and glamorous, with all the social graces.'

'Are you by any chance jealous?'

'Never!' she denied furiously.

'No?' he mocked. 'Then stop it, Jamie. And for the record, I'm not playing games.'

'Aren't you?' she queried bitterly. 'Forgive me if I find that difficult to believe.'

Logan lifted a hand and ran his fingers gently down her cheek, then traced the line of her jaw and came to rest at the edge of her mouth.

'Don't do that,' she said tightly, and he smiled slightly.

'Why? Does it bother you?'

You know it does, she wanted to scream, but she schooled her voice to sound cool and uncaring. 'No.'

'Liar,' he murmured close to her ear. 'I can feel your pulse racing, right here at the base of your throat.' Gently he tilted her chin, turning her face towards him. 'Kiss me, Jamie.'

The breath caught in her throat, temporarily robbing her of speech. 'No,' she refused at last, endeavouring to twist free of him. 'Logan—please!'

'Stay still,' he ordered, not releasing his grip, and she raised storm-tossed eyes to his, anguish and trepidation evident on her expressive features. 'Jamie—a kiss, that's all. You have no need to be afraid of me.'

That's what you think, she thought shakily. I am afraid—of you, but mostly of my own emotions. When you touch me, it's as if I have no control, and it would be so easy to drift into something I'd only hate myself for in the cold light of day.

His head began to descend, and when his lips touched hers she forced herself to remain passive, but it soon became evident that she was fast losing that particular battle, for when he began to apply pressure she opened her own lips with a silent groan of despair, hating herself for being so weak-willed.

It was a long time before he gently extricated her arms from around his neck and cradled her head into the curve of his shoulder. His lips touched her hair, then he lifted her face and kissed her slowly with such a lingering gentleness that it melted her very bones.

'You'd better go inside. If you don't, I might cast aside my few remaining scruples and take you back to my apartment for the night.' He leant forward and opened her door. 'Out, Jamie, before I change my mind.'

'Goodnight, she whispered, totally bemused, and he leaned down and kissed her with bruising intensity.

'Go, for the love of heaven. Tomorrow's Sunday. I'll pick you up at ten and we'll spend the day at the beach.'

She didn't trust herself to speak, and simply nodded in silent acquiescence before slipping out from the car. In the doorway of the flat she stood watching the twin blaze of rear lights disappear, then she moved inside and quietly shut the door behind her. She didn't walk, she floated through the lounge and down the hallway to her bedroom, and it wasn't until she was in bed on the verge of sleep that she remembered she hadn't even thought to check if Susan was home.

The alarm woke Jamie at seven, and she quickly donned a wrap and moved into the kitchen. There was a fresh chicken she had bought at the delicatessen on Friday which she intended to roast so that it would be ready for a picnic lunch, and there were sufficient ingredients for an apple pie. There were some bread rolls in the freezer which she could heat, and together with fresh fruit, it would complete a feast.

At ten to ten the picnic basket was ready, and all she had to do was slip her feet into sandals, brush her hair and push a towel into her bag.

Susan was still asleep, and there was a note cellotaped to her door with the printed words 'do not disturb until at least midday' hastily scrawled. Between their working hours and social life they had scarcely seen each other during the past fortnight. Quickly Jamie unearthed a pen and wrote 'spending the day at beach', then signed her name.

When Logan arrived she was ready, and he eyed the picnic basket with some amusement.

'I guess we've doubled up on food—I should have told you I'd bring everything.'

'That's not fair,' she protested. 'You're taking me out.'

'Stubbornly independent, aren't you?' he teased, taking the basket from her. 'I refuse to waste time arguing. We'll simply go on elsewhere and have whatever is left for dinner.'

'Where are we going to swim?'

'Largs Bay, then we can move towards Brighton. There are several good beaches along the Gulf Saint Vincent—the choice is yours.'

The sun was high in the sky, bathing everything below with a heat that was pleasant, buffeted by a slight breeze from the ocean, and it promised to be a lovely day.

Jamie had elected to wear a one-piece swimsuit of emerald green and had added a wrap-round skirt of matching arnel. Her limbs were already tanned to a deep honey-gold, and with her large-lensed sunglasses she presented an attractive figure as she slid into the car.

The drive to Largs Bay was achieved at a leisurely pace, for Logan took the road that wound round the Gulf, and Jamie viewed the sparkling blue waters with happy expectation. She adored swimming, and somehow the open sea was more inviting than a pool. The tang of salty fresh air, the sand, the feel of the sea on her skin—how she loved it.

The sand was well dotted with beach umbrellas and bodies lying supine and well oiled beneath the hot sun, and from the number of people present it was apparent Largs Bay was a favoured spot.

'The competition is pretty fierce,' Jamie grinned as she carried the picnic basket, her bag and towel over the hot sand, and Logan gave a brief laugh as he walked at her side.

'It isn't the most private place,' he agreed as he deposited the cooler down, then spread out a large rug and secured the beach umbrella. 'However, nobody takes much notice of anyone else. Do you want to sunbathe or swim first?'

'Swim,' she decided unhesitatingly. 'Are you coming in?'

'I'm no water sprite. You go ahead, and I'll join you soon.'

Jamie untied her skirt and slid off her sandals, then placed her sunglasses into her bag. 'Piker,' she grinned at him, wrinkling her nose expressively. 'Swimming is a beneficial exercise.'

His eyes roved over her slim figure with intimate appraisal. 'I can think of better.'

A blush stole over her cheeks, and without a word she turned and ran down over the sand into the water.

It was heavenly, cooling her limbs and caressing her skin like liquid silk, and she struck out with a stylish crawl to get clear of the numerous swimmers playing and cavorting in the shallows. Not too far, an inner voice cautioned, for there was always the danger of sharks, and after a while she turned on her back and floated aimlessly, enjoying the soothing effect of the sun and sea.

'Do you plan on staying here all day?'

Jamie moved her head and met Logan's rugged features creased with amusement close beside her. The water had darkened his hair, and the sight of his muscular shoulders rising above the water sent her nerve-ends tingling alive with sensations that both alarmed and frightened her.

'Is it time for lunch?' she queried guilelessly, and his lips slanted into a mocking smile.

'Do you want to play games, Jamie?'

Her heart lurched crazily, then accelerated at a rapid rate. 'You'd win every time,' she offered faintly. 'But I'll race you to the shore if you like.'

His look was deep and unfathomable, sending goosebumps feathering along her spine, and she shivered slightly.

'You're beautiful, do you know that?' he said softly, and she couldn't think of a single thing to say in reply. 'Let's go in,' he suggested after an interminable silence during which she hadn't been able to tear her eyes away from his.

With a silent nod she turned and began swimming towards the shore, completing two strokes to every one of his, and they stepped out from the sea on to the sand together, her hand becoming lost within his large palm, and she experienced shock at the sight of his athletic well-muscled frame attired in brief black swimming trunks.

So much bared skin and evident raw masculinity embarrassed her, and she kept her eyes averted, cross with herself for the colour she knew must be visible on her cheeks. Fool, she chastised herself mentally—why get into such a tizzy? It was mad—utterly crazy, that he could affect her to such an extent, and she wanted to cry out and plead with him not to amuse himself with her. What she wanted ultimately she didn't dare think about, but it wasn't a brief affair followed by heartbreak. She liked him —almost too much, and she was afraid of letting the friendship continue for fear of what result could come of it.

With concentrated effort Jamie picked up her towel and patted the excess water from her body, then she sat down on the rug and drew on her sunglasses—a welcome protective shield that masked her expressive eyes from view.

'Here, use some of this lotion,' Logan directed, handing a bottle down to her. 'You're well tanned, but the sun is quite fierce—enough to burn.'

Silently she took it and uncapped the slim plastic container then carefully smoothed the lotion onto her legs, her arms, and across the swell of her breasts.

'Let me do your back.'

Jamie passed him the bottle and sat completely still as he soothed the creamy lotion across her shoulders and down over the exposed skin to her waist. His touch was light yet firm, and had a caressing quality that sent her thoughts winging errantly as she imagined what he would be like as a lover. Dynamic, a tiny voice whispered, tantalising, and the temptation to turn her head fractionally and smile at him was almost more than she could bear. Her murmured monosyllabic gratitude emerged from her throat in a husky undertone, then marshalling her wayward senses she turned and leaned towards the picnic basket.

'I hope you haven't brought chicken,' she said brightly, dipping into the sealed containers. 'I guess we should have conferred.'

Logan's smile was easy and without mockery. 'Great minds think alike—chicken it is. Never mind, we'll keep one and take it back to my apartment. Broken into pieces and fried with onions and a dash or curry, it will make a tasty meal.'

Jamie took out paper plates and solemnly handed him one. 'Lettuce and tomato? An egg, celery, and cheese?'

'Trying to feed me up?'

She ignored his raillery. 'Perhaps you'd better help yourself.'

'Hmm,' he murmured teasingly as he foraged among the contents. 'A fruit pie—did you make it?'

'Yes. It's apple, and it's meant for dessert.'

His grin widened and blue eyes gleamed with laughter as he looked at her. 'You sound like a mother—are you telling me I can't have any now?'

'Yes—and I'll rap your hand if you pick at it!'

Something leapt in his eyes. 'I wonder if you'd be so brave if we were alone.'

The fact that they weren't lent her courage. 'I just bet you were an impossible child.'

'I came in for a fair share of punishment, and was rebellious for a brief year or two, as I remember,' he acceded ruminatively. 'I was made painfully aware that any continuance would not be to my advantage.' He withdrew a chicken leg and bit into it with evident enjoyment. 'And you, Jamie—were you a sweet little girl, all sugar and spice?'

She glanced at him beneath her lashes and offered lightly, 'I didn't get the chance to be anything else.'

'Strict parental control?'

'A shade over-protective,' she admitted. 'To enable my self-preservation I had to fly the nest, otherwise I would have been stifled. If I'd had brothers or sisters it would have been all right. As it was, my parents concentrated all their love on me.'

'That was bad?'

She shook her head in silent denial. 'I could never willingly hurt them, but when the chance came to share a working holiday with Susan, they understood I needed to take it. I had to become independent.'

'What if you married and lived some considerable distance from them?'

'That's a possibility I haven't had to consider.'

His eyebrow arched quizzically. 'No proposals of marriage yet?' He shook his head slowly. 'Or hasn't one come along from a man sufficiently well heeled to give you everything?'

'I'm not mercenary. Material things don't necessarily bring happiness.'

'Fine ideals, Jamie,' he drawled cynically. 'Are you trying to tell me you'd choose love first and foremost?'

She met his gaze squarely and held it. 'I couldn't marry a man without it.'

'You don't think that love can change?'

'If the two people concerned work at it and don't take it for granted, it should only grow and flourish. Abused, it couldn't expect to survive for long.'

'So you advocate monogamy?'

'With the right person—yes.'

'Like most females you set the trap with yourself as bait, and wait for an unwary male to happen by?'

Jamie swallowed the angry lump in her throat his hurtful words had caused. 'You're a cynical brute, aren't you, Logan? If you regard marriage as a trap, then you'd be advised never to consider it.'

'Are you really so naïve as to identify the state of matrimony with a picket-fenced cottage, a rose garden, and love guaranteed with every meal?'

'Are you so cynical you can't entertain that there's such a thing as love?' she parried lightly, and his mouth twisted wryly.

'Maybe I learnt my lesson the hard way.'

Jamie looked away, unable to think of any appropriate comment. It took more effort than she

thought possible to steer the conversation on to a
lighter subject. Her smile was forced as she delved
into the picnic basket. 'Some more chicken? A
bread roll?'

'Apple pie?' Logan cajoled with a slight smile,
and she threw him an amusing glance.

'How do you know I'm not the world's worst
cook?'

'You forget I've already sampled a few of your
culinary efforts,' he reminded her sardonically, and
picking up a knife he cut himself a generous slice.

'Have a bite,' he bade, holding it temptingly
close to her mouth, and she obediently bit into the
slice.

'Now I'm going to lie down and sleep it all off,'
she determined ruefully, licking her fingers, then
she wiped them on a tissue she extracted from her
bag.

It was good to close her eyes and be alone with
her thoughts. Logan was far too disturbing for her
peace of mind. She was halfway towards being in
love with him already, and a lot of good that was
going to do her!

The sun heated her limbs and began to burn,
and she eased herself over on to her back. That was
better. In half an hour she would slip into the sea
to cool off.

CHAPTER NINE

'HEY, princess—wake up!'

Jamie came to with a start as a warm mouth covered hers, and she blinked rapidly as Logan's face swam into focus.

'You've had enough sun for one day,' he smiled down at her. 'Another swim, then I think we'll head for the botanic gardens.'

She sat up slowly and stretched her arms. 'What time is it?'

'After three.'

'Are you coming in?'

He inclined his head and stood to his feet, and towering above her, then leaned down and offered her his hand.

The sand was hot beneath her bare feet, and after a few steps she began to run towards the sea. Logan reached the water first and plunged in, then surfaced and watched as she walked out to where he stood.

They swam with leisurely strokes, then headed back to shore. It took no more than ten minutes for their swimsuits to dry, and Logan collected their gear, leaving Jamie to carry the picnic basket and her bag. Back at the car he pulled on grey suede trousers and slipped on a shirt, then he stowed everything in the trunk.

The remainder of the afternoon passed in a hazy glow, and as they wandered hand-in-hand around the botanic gardens in the inner city she viewed the splendid array of flowers and shrubs with a sense of pleasant detachment. It had been a thoroughly enjoyable day, and it hadn't finished, for there was still the evening ahead.

It was almost six o'clock when Logan eased the car into the steady stream of traffic and began heading through the city streets until he reached Glenelg, drawing to a halt in the driveway of a mature double-storied home overlooking the beach.

Jamie viewed it dubiously, for it wasn't what she had expected—although Logan himself was something of an enigma. Picturing his apartment and where it might be situated, she had imagined a small self-contained unit—certainly nothing as grand or as large as this.

It occupied the entire upper level of the architecturally re-structured home, and she could only admire the modern features—sloping beamed ceilings, pine-timbered walls, the wide picture windows facing out over the beach. Designed on an open plan, the effect was cool and spacious, and bore the visible signs of an interior decorator, for everything blended with splendid co-ordination from the muted drapes to the cushion-covered furniture, the sheepskin scatter-rugs on the slate-paving effect vinyl flooring. Imitation lanterns hung suspended on chains from the ceiling, and the lounge was equipped with a stereo, television, and several shelves filled with books.

Logan indicated a hallway leading off from the dining-room. 'The bathroom is down to the left if you'd like a shower.'

'Thank you,' she acknowledged politely, and without a further word she crossed the room and stepped down the hall.

The bathroom took her breath away, for its walls were covered entirely with synthetic marble in startling black and white, and there was a sunken tiled bath, a shower, and gold-framed mirrors that reflected the room's elegant fittings.

Jamie took off her skirt and swimsuit and slipped beneath the warm jet of water, then she quickly rinsed her hair of the effects of sea water, and emerged to wrap herself in one of the huge fluffy towels reposing neatly folded on a nearby stool.

Her toilette completed, she delved into her bag and extracted pants, then secured her skirt and tied on the matching wrap-around top. Her hair felt clean and would soon dry, even wound into a coil on top of her head. A swift application of moisturising cream, a touch of lipstick, and she was ready.

Logan was in the kitchen deftly dissecting chicken flesh from its bones, and there was an appetising aroma of fried onions coming from the electric frying pan.

'Would you like me to do that?' Jamie asked, crossing to his side, and he speared her with a look of quizzical amusement.

'Don't you think I'm competent?'

'Of course. I thought you might want to shower, that's all.'

'In that case, the kitchen's yours for five minutes,' he conceded, and she took the fork he handed her and began adding chicken to the simmering curry and onions.

'You'll find plates and cutlery,' he informed her, sweeping an arm towards a set of drawers and cupboards. 'Help yourself.' With that he moved easily towards the hallway and disappeared from sight.

Jamie busied herself setting the table, making a passable salad from the contents of Logan's picnic contributions, and then switched on the oven to heat the bread rolls.

'Hmm, that smells good,' a voice drawled from behind her, and she threw him a swift smile. 'There's some wine in the refrigerator—somehow, I think beer would be infinitely lacking as a suitable complement.'

The food was delicious, and followed by fresh fruit and cheese, it was one of the most enjoyable meals Jamie had eaten in a long time.

'Coffee?' Logan queried mildly as he leaned back in his chair, and Jamie stood to her feet and began gathering dishes together.

'Leave those,' he directed indolently, but she shook her head.

'I'll do them while we're waiting for the coffee.'

'My guests are usually content to leave the dishes in the sink,' he mused, and she looked at him with uncertainty.

'If you'd rather——'

'Jamie!' he chastised with an expressive sigh. 'For the love of heaven—do the dishes, by all means, if it will ease your conscience.'

She should be a sophisticate like the women of his acquaintance, she decided, and ignore domesticity for an after-dinner drink and the sharing of scintillating conversation—even drift towards the bedroom as the natural end to a pleasantly spent day. Instead, she could only present herself as an immature gauche girl whose nerves shredded at the very thought of sharing sexual intimacies. In today's permissive society she was a pitied oddity!

With dedicated concentration she carried the dishes across to the kitchen, filled the sink with hot sudsy water, then carefully transferred plates, glasses and cutlery clean and sparkling into the draining-rack. Now for the frying pan, and the chore would be completed.

'The water is bubbling itself into oblivion,'

Logan remarked close behind her, and she raised her head in consternation as he leaned forward and closed the switch.

'I'm sorry, I didn't——'

'Shut up,' he directed quietly, and she felt his fingers unfasten the pins securing her hair, then its length uncoiled and fell loosely about her shoulders. His fingers threaded through it gently, spreading it out, and she felt her breath catch when he murmured, 'I've been wanting to do that for the past hour.'

'I've only the frying pan to finish,' she began, and he cursed briefly.

'To hell with the frying pan!' His head bent down to her shoulder, and she felt his lips touch her neck, then travel up the sensitive cord to nuzzle an earlobe.

Hands drew her away from the sink back against him, then slid down over her shoulders to cup each breast, and she uttered a gasp as they slid beneath the silky material.

'Logan,' she protested, but it was too late, for the ties were undone, and she gave a groan of despair as he turned her towards him.

His lips were warm and persuasive, his hands gently caressing, and after a few timeless seconds she became lost, totally mindless beneath the disruptive sensuality of his touch.

She was drowning in her own emotions, almost beyond caring, when warning bells triggered inside her brain, bringing her up from the depths and returning sanity.

Dear God, what was she thinking of! She had to be mad—stark raving mad! Unbidden, of their own volition, her eyes filled with tears that overflowed and spilled slowly down each cheek, and she stood passively, unable to respond.

Slowly Logan raised his head, and she regarded him silently through a watery mist. Her mouth began to tremble uncontrollably, and he uttered a husky oath.

'Tears—woman's ultimate weapon,' he derided softly, and his eyes darkened measurably. 'Jamie, for the love of heaven, why are you crying?' His voice was silk-smooth and dangerous.

'Please—I can't stay. I have to go home.' She glanced down and blushed at the sight of her breasts, burgeoned and exposed, their nipples taut. Shakily she searched for the ties that would draw the material across, but the erotic memory of his mouth caused her such agitation she was incapable of successfully securing a knot.

Firmly her hands were pushed aside, and within seconds the ties were fastened.

'I'll get my bag,' she said slowly, almost stumbling over the words, and she shivered involuntarily despite the heat. 'Don't worry about taking me home—I'll get a taxi—a bus. It doesn't matter,' she finished miserably, and turned away from him and walked towards the door.

It wasn't until she was outside in the driveway that she realised Logan was behind her, and she gave a startled cry when he unlocked the car and tossed her bag on to the front seat.

'I——'

'Let's walk,' he interrupted brusquely, relocking the door. He caught hold of her hand in a merciless grip that brought a protesting gasp of pain from her lips, but the pressure didn't ease as he led her across the road and on to the grassy apron that led down to the beach.

It was dusk, almost dark, and street lights were reflected on the water, mirroring a delicate tracery of yellow-white pinpoint illumination. Sounds of children playing as they endeavoured to make the most of the fast-fading light disrupted the air, and there were people strolling in groups enjoying the evening dusk.

Jamie walked beside him in silence—a silence that grew more formidable with every passing minute. She wanted to pull free and run—anywhere, away from him. Tentatively she tugged her hand, but the pressure increased to such a degree she cried out for fear her bones might snap.

Instantly she was free, and his muffled apology barely registered as he lifted her hand to his lips, then his arm encircled her shoulders drawing her close to his side, and he shortened his steps to match hers, leading the way down to the water's edge.

How far they walked she had little idea, for it could easily have been a mile or two before Logan eventually turned and they began retracing their steps. Several times she started to speak, but no words found voice, and after a while she surrendered to the silence, unwilling to sever the tenuous thread that bound them together.

When they reached the driveway Logan unlocked the passenger door and held it open. Jamie stood poised, uncertain whether she should get inside, and he leaned forward.

'I'm taking you home.' His voice was hard and inflexible. 'Now, get in, and for God's sake—don't argue.'

The drive from Glenelg to her flat at Henley Beach was achieved in a short time, and as soon as the car came to a halt Jamie reached for the door-clasp.

'I'll call you tomorrow,' Logan declared brusquely, and she wasn't capable of emitting so much as a word; even goodbye would have choked her.

She almost ran up the path leading to the front door, and she unlocked it quickly and escaped inside, closing it behind her without once looking back.

'Jamie?'

Susan—she was home, and if she saw her looking like this she would guess something was wrong. Quickly Jamie raked fingers through her hair, then drawing a deep breath she walked down towards the kitchen.

'Hi—— I was just about to make coffee,' Susan greeted brightly. 'Care for a cup?'

'Please—I'd love some,' Jamie responded gratefully, and her smile was a little forced as she met Susan's inquisitive gaze.

'Hey, you look——' Susan deliberated carefully, 'slightly bothered,' she finished slowly. 'Are you?'

Jamie sank down into a chair and leant her elbows on the table. 'It's a long story,' she intimated wryly.

'Logan?' the other girl hazarded. 'You've been going out with him, haven't you? Okay, so what's the problem? Is he giving you a hard time?'

'*Yes*, and yes again,' Jamie acquiesced ruefully. 'It would be so easy, and yet I can't.'

'You mean you haven't——? Susan's consternation was almost comical.

'It's not funny.'

Susan quickly masked her incredulity. 'No, it's not in the least funny,' she declared with sobriety. 'What happens next?'

Jamie grimaced, and rested her chin into her cupped hands. 'I guess it's "goodbye, Logan".'

'Has he said so?'

'No. He said he'd call me, but I'll probably never hear from him again.'

Susan looked pensive for a few minutes. 'Do you

want to head on for Melbourne? Between us, we've got enough money for the trip, and we should get a job without too much trouble.'

'Logan lives in Melbourne,' Jamie told her. 'He just stays in Adelaide occasionally. I'd be jumping from the frying pan into the fire.'

'But you don't want to see him again—right?' The sound of water boiling captured Susan's attention and she disconnected the kettle, made the coffee and carried the two mugs to the table.

'I only know things can't go on as they are,' Jamie said quietly. With considerable effort she glanced across the table at her friend. 'For the past few weeks it's been a case of "hello—goodbye". What's been happening in your world? How's the job?'

Successfully diverted, Susan enthused about Richard, the places they had been, and glossed over her employment as being necessary, but bearable.

'Well, I'm for bed,' Susan declared, stifling a yawn. 'I have to be up at the crack of dawn. See you in the morning.'

Jamie raised a hand, then drained the rest of her coffee. She didn't feel in the least like sleeping, and she decided to write a letter home, then read for a while.

Monday was a day like any other working day, with the exception that when Jamie finished at two-thirty Logan was nowhere in sight. Not that she really expected to see him after last night. She even waited outside the restaurant's main entrance for ten minutes in case he had been delayed, then gave up and headed towards the Festival Centre where she filled in time admiring the splendid architecture of the theatres and sat beneath the shade of a tree in the adjacent grounds leafing through a magazine she'd bought.

At precisely five o'clock she reported for work, and the early part of the evening was remarkably slow, not picking up until after eight when a group arrived demanding food and attention, so that the following hour seemed to pass in a flurry of activity.

'You're wanted on the phone, *chérie*,' Georges intimated quietly as he paused between tables, momentarily capturing her attention. 'Be brief, if you do not wish to anger our mutual employer. He does not approve of personal calls during the hours of business. I will cover you for a few minutes.'

Jamie nodded and hurried into the kitchen where she picked up the receiver. The noise forbade privacy, and she placed a hand over one ear in an attempt to hear after she had identified herself.

'Jamie? What in the name of heaven is that noise?'

Logan! Her heart flipped, then began to beat erratically. 'I'm taking the call in the kitchen,' she explained. 'What do you want?'

'There's a party I should attend tonight,' he said without preamble. 'I'll collect you after work.'

'Are you asking, or telling me?' she queried, and heard his husky laugh.

'Will you come?'

'I'll have to call in to the flat first,' she warned. 'The clothes I've worn to work aren't suitable.'

'Fine—I'll be waiting.'

At a quick glance from Georges, Jamie said swiftly, 'Logan, I'll have to go—we're busy. See you later.' A smile lit her expressive features as she replaced the receiver, and the remainder of the evening seemed to fly, so that in seemingly no time at all she was emerging on to the main street to find Logan waiting outside.

'Hi,' she greeted him a trifle breathlessly, becoming startlingly aware of the powerful masculinity he exuded, and aware of the sudden tightening of her stomach muscles as he smiled down at her.

Without a word he took hold of her arm and led her towards the car, and when she was seated inside he moved round behind the wheel and set the vehicle heading towards Henley Beach.

For the sake of something to say, Jamie broached, 'What sort of party is it—formal? And where?'

The look he cast her held a tinge of amusement that was apparent in his voice. 'Informal, Jamie, at a friend's apartment not far from my own. You sound mildly apprehensive. Are you?'

'Should I be?' she countered, and he responded smoothly,

'Not in the least.'

As they entered the flat she glanced back over her shoulder. 'Have I time for a quick shower? I promise I won't be long.'

'Go ahead. Mind if I use the phone?'

'Help yourself.' She swept a hand towards the dining-room, then moved towards her bedroom. Quickly discarding clothes, she showered, then hastily inspected the contents of her wardrobe. Informal could mean anything from casual attire to sophisticated simple elegance. After a few minutes of indecision she chose a silky halter-style dress of deep gold, swept her hair into an elegantly-contrived knot on top of her head, applied make-up, highlighting her eyes, then slid her bare feet into slim-heeled sandals and slid a make-up purse, some money and her keys into an evening bag.

The appreciative gleam evident in Logan's dark

blue eyes as she entered the lounge sent her spirits soaring, and she gave a quick twirl in the centre of the room. 'Will I do?'

For an answer he leant out and caught hold of her arm, pulling her irresistibly forward until only a few inches separated them. His head lowered as his arms enfolded her slim curves against his hardened frame, then his mouth was on hers, hungry and intensely erotic as he remorselessly brought alive an answering ardency, so that when he reluctantly put her aside she stood regarding him silently, her breathing ragged.

Jamie's eyes were eloquent pools mirroring bemusement, and she drew a steadying breath as his fingers trailed gently across her sensitive kiss-swollen lips, then tautened involuntarily as his fingertips slid down her throat to the cleft between her breasts.

'Would you be shocked if I said I'd like to kiss every square inch of you?' Logan queried softly, following the trail of his fingers with his lips. 'And delight in having you kiss me—teach you to please me, as I can please you?'

Jamie felt her knees weaken and turn to water at the latent sensuality evident in his voice, his touch, and her heart quickened, its beat thudding until it seemed to deafen her ears.

'Logan!' Her voice came out as a strangled gasp, and she began to tremble until her whole body shook with suppressed emotion. 'Please—the party! Shouldn't we be leaving?'

Slowly he raised his head, and she almost died at the naked desire evident in his darkened, passionate gaze. Then the edges of his mouth lifted slightly, curving his lips into a faintly rueful smile. 'This time you win,' he teased gently, planting a brief hard kiss on her mouth, then he uttered a soft laugh, his eyes vivid and gleaming wickedly. 'You haven't a vestige of lipstick left.'

Shakily Jamie withdrew her make-up purse from her bag and attempted to effect repairs, although her hand was far from steady, and after a few seconds Logan plucked the gold-encased tube from her fingers. Lifting her chin, he stroked colour over the fulness of her lips, regarding his efforts with a faint teasing smile, then he placed the lipstick back into her purse.

'Everything back to normal.'

Normal? How could anything be normal ever again? Jamie wondered dazedly as she followed him to the car, and she sat in reflective silence as the vehicle sped towards their destination.

In the graciously-furnished lounge of their host's beach-front home Jamie allowed her gaze to wander idly over the assortment of guests present, perceiving at a glance that all the women bore an air of moneyed sophistication, for although informal, their attire fairly cried the exclusive individuality of top model brand-labels, their hair was expensively coiffured, their make-up superb.

'I'll get you a drink,' Logan declared, letting his arm drop from about her waist. 'What would you like?'

'Something long and cool—and not too strong,' she said quietly, and glimpsed his wry smile.

'In case you need to keep your wits about you?' he taunted gently. 'Relax, Jamie—I wouldn't harm a hair on your head.'

'It's not my—head I'm worried about,' she said tremulously after an infinite pause, and he uttered a silent laugh.

'My dear sweet Jamie,' he mocked softly, his eyes strangely serious, 'believe me when I assure you

you have nothing to worry about. I'll get you that drink.'

Shortly after he returned to her side she caught a flash of silver-blonde hair and seconds later recognised Sacha Andreas. She was powerless against the curling muscles as her stomach tensed into a tight painful ball, and she had to physically force herself to smile as the stunningly alluring figure wended its way towards them.

Looking like a model straight out of the pages of a top fashion magazine Sacha wafted over—literally, as the aura of French perfume, Lanvin's *My Sin*, Jamie perceived, preceded her.

'Logan, you gorgeous man—you made it!' Sacha greeted with avid enthusiasm, ignoring Jamie completely. 'I was sure you would.' She gave a light tinkling laugh as she glanced down at the glass in her hand. 'Darling, would you mind? Vodka and tonic, a dash of bitters, and ice.'

Logan gave a practised smile, his eyes vividly blue as he flicked Jamie a piercing glance. 'You remember Sacha?'

Remember? How could she forget! A little green monster rose to the fore, lending her dark brown eyes an involuntary momentary glitter, then politeness forced her to acknowledge the Greek girl's penetrating stare.

'If you'll excuse me?' Logan interposed, then he was gone, leaving Jamie alone and peculiarly vulnerable.

'A little piece of advice—you don't mind, do you?' Sacha pouted the instant Logan was out of earshot. 'It won't do you any good to chase after Logan. He's some man,' she added in a voice soft as silk, 'but never yours. So——' she paused delicately, and Jamie finished sweetly,

'Hands off?'

'Clever girl,' the other accorded. 'I'm so glad you understand.'

'Oh, I understand perfectly,' Jamie declared solemnly, and Sacha smiled.

'He's way out of your class—but then you know that, don't you?'

'Whatever you say,' Jamie agreed in a droll voice, and the other girl gave a seductive laugh.

'So sensible of you to decide not to fight me for him.'

'I don't believe in war,' Jamie responded ambiguously. 'But I rather think the ultimate decision rests with Logan.' For a moment she thought Sacha was going to strike her, then the angry eyes lost their venomous gleam, and the reason was instantly apparent as Logan returned.

His hand reached out and caught hold of Jamie's, spreading her fingers as he threaded his own through hers, and his touch was reassuring.

'Dance with me?' The look he cast down was infinitely solemn, his eyes penetrating as they glimpsed the faint tension evident, and when she was in his arms and moving slowly to the music he queried, 'Sacha bothers you?'

Flippancy was the only way to deal with it, she decided wryly. 'Should she?'

'No.' Logan's tone was blunt, almost angry, and she gave an inaudible gasp as his grip tightened with painful intensity. Then suddenly aware of his strength he released her and uttered an exclamation of self-disgust, pulling her close and resting his cheek down against her head.

A terrible lethargy assailed her limbs, rendering her boneless, and it was with considerable reluctance that she drew away from him when the dance came to an end.

Logan rarely left her side for what remained of

the evening, and each and every one of Sacha's attempts to commandeer him—and there were several—were met with brusque restraint. Jamie inwardly cringed, sure that if he should ever treat her in a like manner she would curl up and die.

'Let's get out of here,' Logan declared at last, and Jamie saw with surprise that it was after two o'clock.

In the car driving back to her flat she was strangely silent, reflecting on Sacha's barbs and possessiveness with something akin to mild jealousy, then grimaced in the darkness. There was nothing mild about it! She wanted to rage and scream like a primitive cat! The feeling frightened her, that and knowing she was capable of such violence. To be jealous, you had to care deeply, and she knew with sickening certainty that Logan was her life, the very air she breathed. Faced with the prospect of living without him made her want to die. And what of him? He desired her, that much she knew—but as for anything more, even a lasting relationship, much less marriage, she didn't dare contemplate.

'Tired?'

Jamie came out of her reverie, realising with a start that the car was stationary outside her apartment. 'No,' she denied, contrite. 'Just lost in thought.'

'Anything you want to talk about?'

She shook her head slowly, and he leaned forward, sliding a hand along the back of her seat until it rested at her nape, the fingers beginning an idle caress that sent shivers scudding down her spine. Gently he reached for the knot of hair atop her head, releasing the pins that held it in place, then when it fell in a swathe about her shoulders he threaded his fingers through it as if the action afforded him pleasure.

'Come here,' he instructed gently, and of its own volition her body swayed towards him, mindless and blindly obedient. 'Kiss me, Jamie.'

She gazed at him wordlessly, momentarily at a loss, then she raised her face slightly and pressed her lips against the edge of his mouth, feeling them part beneath her own, silently encouraging her to initiate the exploration. She felt his response and began kissing him with a fervour that set alight hidden fires deep within until her veins sang as the heat coursed through her body. Then subtly it altered as he took command, charging her with an emotion so tumultuous she cried out as the agonising ache demanded fulfilment.

'Jamie,' Logan groaned huskily against her throat. 'This has got to go on—or stop. If you're just playing at being a temptress, then I warn you —I'm hovering on the brink of no return. If Susan is going to be in the flat, we'll go back to my apartment. Which is it to be?'

His words acted like a dash of cold water, and Jamie dragged herself away from him, pushing him at arm's length. 'I have to go in,' she said shakily. 'Alone.'

'Jamie—for the love of heaven!' His voice was an emotive growl, and she shivered at the depth of leashed passion evident.

'Logan, I want to, but I can't. I just can't!' she whispered brokenly, close to tears. 'I'm sorry.' Her hand reached out for the door-clasp as she hastily sought to escape.

'Damn you, Jamie,' he cursed huskily, his expression savage in the dim light. 'Have you any idea what you're doing to me?'

'And me—have you given any thought about that?' she countered shakily. 'I've got feelings, too.' Then she was out of the car and running, stumbling up the path to the front door.

Somehow she managed to insert the key, then she was inside, leaning against the closed door, gasping in huge painful breaths of air, unsure whether to laugh or cry, and close to tearful hysteria.

She half expected Logan to follow her, and she listened fearfully for his footsteps and the sound of his voice on the other side of the door.

After interminable minutes her ears did catch a slight sound, but it was the engine starting up, followed quickly by a steadily decreasing purr as the car drove away.

CHAPTER TEN

THE following day dragged by so slowly that Jamie was beginning to wonder if the clock hadn't suddenly decided to behave with temperamental disregard so that each minute seemed to become an hour, and after a restless, sleepless night she woke on Wednesday morning to the insistent ringing of the telephone.

Muttering beneath her breath, she buried her head under the pillow, hoping that Susan would answer it, then tossed the pillow aside as it continued to ring, giving a groan of despair as she remembered her friend would already have left for work.

'Hello,' she murmured indistinctly.

'Jamie? How are you?' When she didn't answer, Logan's voice sharpened. 'Jamie, are you there?'

'Hello, Logan,' she responded carefully.

'I've had to return to Melbourne,' he said without preamble. 'How soon can you pack?'

'I beg your pardon?'

'You heard,' he said wryly. 'How soon can you pack and get on a plane?'

Her heart began an erratic tattoo. 'Are you serious?'

'Perfectly. How long? A day—two?'

'Why?' she asked baldly, and heard his audible sigh of impatience.

'Must I spell it out?'

'I think you'd better,' Jamie said slowly, her stomach beginning to perform a series of painful acrobatics.

'I want you here with me. Is that plain enough?'

'Not entirely. I can't see what difference it would make.'

'My God, I could shake you,' he declared bluntly. 'I'm proposing, dammit!'

For a moment she couldn't speak. 'What kind of proposal?'

'The "ring on your finger" kind. For want of a better word—marriage.'

'You can't mean that,' she managed at last, her voice shaking uncontrollably.

'Can't I?' Logan mocked. 'Well, Jamie, are you going to let me make an honest woman of you?'

'You expect me to give you an answer now?'

'Do you need to think about it?' he queried softly, and she shook her head.

'No,' she denied slowly.

'I'll organise everything this end and ring you tomorrow morning,' he stated firmly. 'In the meantime, hand in your notice and start packing.'

'Logan——' she began protestingly, and he interrupted gently,

'I love you, Jamie. The rest of it will have to keep until you get here.'

'Logan, I can't leave yet. There's my job—and Susan——'

'Jamie, I'll call you tomorrow.'

'I haven't said yes,' she wailed despairingly, and heard him chuckle softly.

'Then say it. Repeat after me—"yes, Logan, I'll marry you".'

'How can you be so sure?' she asked.

His answer was definite. 'I've been fighting it ever since you appeared out of the middle of nowhere—a pint-sized scrap of femininity that knocked me sideways.'

'Then it's yes,' she decided, her heart in her voice.

There was silence for a few seconds, then he said quietly, 'We'll be married here just as soon as I can arrange a licence.'

'We can't possibly,' she spluttered, awed at the way he was sweeping her along. 'My parents— they'd be dreadfully upset if they weren't there. I can't——'

Logan intervened gently. 'Put a call through to-day and tell your parents. Give me their number and I'll speak to your father.' His voice became openly teasing. 'Think about where you'd like to go for a honeymoon.'

'You're going too fast,' Jamie protested faintly, and he gave a husky laugh.

'Not fast enough, believe me!'

A sudden thought occurred to her. 'How can I tell my parents about you?' she asked slowly. 'I don't even know your surname,' she ended, aghast at how little she knew of him.

'Jordan—Logan Jordan, Jamie. I'm thirty-five, and I can comfortably provide for your needs.'

'This is ridiculous!' Hot tears seared her eyes, and the hand holding the receiver began to shake.

'Jamie,' he berated softly, 'you're marrying *me* —the statistics are a mere appendage.' He cursed briefly. 'For the love of God, you're not crying, are you?'

'No, of course not,' she denied, her voice wobbly with suppressed emotion.

'Jamie!' he warned huskily, and she quickly gathered together a measure of control.

'This call must be expensive,' she said swiftly, and he waved it aside with blunt brusqueness.

'Give me your parents' number, Jamie. I'll put a call through myself.'

She gave it to him, then began uncertainly, 'Logan—'

'Jamie, get a pen, there's a good girl,' he bade quietly. 'I'll give you the number here, and I want you to put through a collect call as soon as you get in from work tonight.'

"But that will be close to eleven-thirty,' she protested, and heard his wry laugh.

'I don't go to bed early—now, have you got that pen handy?'

She nodded silently, then realised he couldn't see her. 'Yes.' She wrote down the series of digits.

'It would be advisable to contact your parents before I do,' Logan suggested, and she offered shakily.

'I'll ring them before I go in to work.'

'Good girl!' His voice was warm and sent shivers feathering down her spine. 'I'll wait for your call tonight—meantime, take care,' he said gently.

'Yes.' Her voice seemed to choke in her throat. 'You, too.' She replaced the receiver carefully, then sat staring into space for a long time, unable to believe that he loved her—actually *loved* her. There was no need to examine her own feelings, but marriage was something she hadn't dared contemplate.

A glance at her watch showed that she had half an hour before she must leave for work, and if she was to telephone her parents she would have to do it now. The time difference meant she was sure to catch them at home now. Quickly she placed the call and was fortunate to get through almost immediately.

Jamie spoke to her mother first, and after the initial surprise she took the news very well, then her father came on the line. It was all too brief, and she promised to ring again the following day.

The hours sped swiftly as Jamie went about her

work in a state of euphoria, and it was twenty past eleven when she parked the station wagon outside the flat, locked it, then walked up the path to the front door.

As she drew out the key a lengthy frame unfolded itself from the shadows and moved into the dim moonlight.

'Oh!' she cried out, then recognition brought forth a startled gasp. 'Logan, what are you doing here?'

'You could sound a bit more enthusiastic,' he chided with amusement, taking the key from her nerveless fingers and fitting it into the lock.

'I thought you were going to phone,' Jamie protested, shaken by his unexpected presence.

'Shall we go inside?' he quizzed. 'I've no particular desire to conduct this conversation on the doorstep.'

'Of course,' she concurred apologetically, and when the door closed he pulled her close, kissing her with a thoroughness that rendered her completely breathless.

'Why did you come?' she asked, her whole body quivering from the response he evoked.

His smile did strange things to her equilibrium, and she caught hold of his arms to support herself. 'Because I couldn't stay away,' he revealed, and he lifted a hand to smooth back a stray tendril of her long hair. 'You sounded apprehensive and overwhelmed when I rang this morning. I wasn't sure that by the time you'd had time to think, you might have imagined any number of reasons why you couldn't marry me.' His eyes lit with humour as his fingers slid down to tilt her chin. 'I thought you might be in need of a little reassurance and decided to deliver it personally. Any objections?'

Jamie let her tongue run over her lips, unaware

of the provocativeness such an action afforded. 'No, none.'

Logan withdrew a small jewellers box from his jacket pocket and handed it to her. 'Open it, Jamie,' he directed solemnly.

She took it from him with shaking fingers and snapped open the tiny clasp, then gave a nearly inaudible cry that was a mixture of pleasure and awe. 'Logan, it's beautiful!' she gasped as he slipped the square-cut diamond solitaire from its velvet bed, and taking hold of her left hand he slid the ring on to her finger.

'Thank you,' she breathed tremulously, and reaching up she planted a shy kiss at the edge of his mouth.

'I've obtained a licence,' he slanted musingly, 'and made arrangements for us to be married on Monday.'

'This Monday?' she queried, startled.

'*Yes*, Jamie,' he mocked gently. 'Have you nothing to say?'

'I can't think properly,' she offered shakily.

'Next, your parents—I contacted them early this evening, then again a little over an hour ago. They intend flying over at the weekend,' he finished drolly.

'Logan, it's happening too quickly,' Jamie protested.

'It's only just begun,' he informed her with a quizzical smile. 'I'm taking you back to Melbourne with me in the morning.'

'I can't—I haven't told Susan,' she began in anguish. 'There's my job—I've told them I'm leaving, but not *when*. How can I—'

He silenced her effectively, beginning a slow evocative exploration of her mouth that blotted out everything save the sensuality of his touch, the deep all-consuming passion evident between them.

At last he lifted his head to gaze down at her, his eyes more vividly blue than she had ever seen them. 'You can, easily,' he assured her gently. 'I'll contact your employer first thing tomorrow morning—Susan I'll leave to you. I want you with me, Jamie, not hundreds of miles away in another State.'

'I—I'll tell Susan before she leaves for work tomorrow morning. My parents seem quite happy about—us,' she faltered slightly, and Logan intervened swiftly, teasingly,

'Hey, this is a wedding we're planning, not a wake! Don't you want to marry me?'

Jamie drew a gulping breath, then smiled, her lips trembling. 'Yes.' Of that she was certain—it was just the details and arrangements that bothered her.

'For a moment I thought you might be having reservations,' he said lightly, and she gave a breathless laugh.

'What time do we leave tomorrow?'

'We're due at the airport at midday.'

'Logan, I haven't even began to pack!' she wailed

'It's quite simple,' he declared solemnly. 'You just open suitcases and throw everything in. Ten minutes should take care of it.' Her scandalised expression brought forth a gleam of amusement. 'Jamie, we'll do it together. But first, how about a drink?' He smiled down at her. 'I brought champagne—it's appropriate, don't you think?'

An hour later Jamie's bedroom looked as if a tornado had swept through it, and after two glasses of champagne she was beyond caring how the packing was completed and quite happy to leave the bulk of it to Logan. It seemed to work, for in no time at all two suitcases and an overnight bag stood near the door, and apart from her immediate needs all the drawers lay empty.

'Coffee—then bed,' Jamie declared with a prodigious yawn.

'Hmm, let's dispense with the coffee,' Logan murmured, pulling her into his arms.

'Are you staying at your apartment?' she queried, and he gave a husky chuckle.

'How about here?'

Her stomach flipped, then tightened painfully. 'Logan, there's the couch in the lounge——'

'Couch—hell!' His hands slid up her arms to grasp hold of her shoulders. 'Jamie, in the name of God,' he groaned.

She gazed up at him in silence, afraid and apprehensive. 'You can't stay here. Not—not in the way you mean.'

'The hell I can't,' he swore softly, his eyes narrowing as he glimpsed the tears welling behind her eyes. 'Jamie, I love you, dammit! In five days we'll be married.'

She drew a deep shuddering breath, capitulating with a sense of fatalism. 'If—if that's what you want.'

'Jamie!' Hard hands shook her, and she cried out.

'Logan, please!' Two tears overflowed and ran slowly down each cheek. 'I can't fight against you any more.'

'For the love of heaven!' he cursed violently. 'Why should you fight me?'

In silence she looked up at him, seeing the angry puzzlement evident, and she lifted a hand to her trembling lips, then shakily brushed her cheeks. 'I haven't—slept with anyone before.'

His sharp indrawn breath made her blink. 'Are

you telling me the truth?' he demanded savagely, and her eyes widened, mirroring hurt that he should disbelieve her, and her voice choked in her throat.

'Why should I lie?'

He looked down at her intently for seemingly interminable minutes, then the muscles tautened along his jaw as he lifted his hand and ran his fingers gently down her cheek. 'Oh God,' he groaned audibly. 'Jamie Prentiss, I love you,' he said softly, his mouth curving into a slanting smile as he tilted her chin. 'Come and see me to the door.'   He bent down and bestowed a gentle lingering kiss, then moved away, catching hold of her hand. 'I'll pick you up around eleven in the morning.'

At the front door he lifted her hand to his lips, then released it and walked out to where a car stood parked a short distance down the road.

After talking to Susan over an early breakfast, Jamie felt more at ease, for the other girl was genuinely delighted with the news, and dismissed Jamie's apologies for not being able to complete their working holiday as originally planned.

At eleven o'clock Jamie stood ready and waiting, her suitcases standing just inside the front door. She cast a careful glance over the flat, conducting a last-minute check that everything was as it should be, and as she crossed back into the lounge there was a quick staccato knock on the door.

'Hi,' she greeted quietly, endeavouring to still the way her heart leapt at the sight of the man standing with indolent ease in the open doorway. Attired in casual dark brown trousers, a pin-striped shirt left unbuttoned at the neck with the cuffs turned back to reveal muscular forearms, he looked refreshed and indomitably male.

'Ready?'

His smile did strange things to her composure, and when he leaned down to brush her lips with his own she had to restrain herself from flinging her arms up around his neck.

Logan stowed her luggage in the trunk of the car while Jamie slipped into the passenger seat, and as he slid in beside her she turned towards him with a slight frown.

'Did you phone the restaurant?'

'All taken care of,' Logan reassured her, slipping a hand into his pocket and tossing a sealed envelope on to her lap. 'Your wages.'

'I didn't think I'd be entitled to any, leaving so suddenly,' she exclaimed.

'You can go on a mad shopping spree,' he teased, and she laughed.

'I shall have to! Do you realise I have to buy something to get married in, and countless other things—all within the space of a few hours tomorrow?' She turned slightly, wrinkling her nose at him. 'Being swept off my feet is one thing, but I'm beginning to see the advantages of a conventional engagement—at least it gives a girl time to prepare!'

'Prepare be damned,' Logan teased unmercifully, and she poked out her tongue.

'Hmm—that's typical of a man. There's one thing uppermost in your mind—and nobody needs more than one guess to know what that is!'

The look he cast her was brief and penetrating as he negotiated the traffic. 'Not entirely—although I can't deny I want you, physically. The usual reasons for an engagement of any length don't apply. I already have suitable accommodation,' he informed her indolently. 'Sufficient money to support you. We're both sure—so why wait?'

Put like that Jamie couldn't help but agree, and the remainder of the drive to the airport and the subsequent

They were met at Tullamarine airport by a man whom Logan introduced as his personal secretary, Mark Hamilton, who efficiently dealt with their luggage and escorted them to a sleek Audi sedan before slipping behind the wheel.

Melbourne's streets were wide and tree-lined, giving the impression of spaciousness. Green and yellow-painted streetcars provided a distinctive feature, their clacking sound as they traversed the steel tracks adding another dimension to the inner-city noise.

'Not long now,' Logan intimated quietly, leaning towards her, informing her, 'My apartment is in Kew.'

A slight feeling of uncertainty trickled down Jamie's spine as the car slowed down and turned in to a wide curving driveway, then swept past the imposing mutli-storied apartment building down into an underground garage.

She grew more apprehensive with every passing second as they emerged from the car and ascended by private key-operated elevator to the uppermost floor, and the faint disturbing sensation inside her stomach began to magnify alarmingly as the doors swished open and Logan ushered her into a sumptuous foyer.

Beyond a massive oak-panelled door her first impression was of pale oyster-coloured thick shag-pile carpet, sofas covered in luxurious dark brown velvet, neutral walls relieved by several prints and ornamental light fittings. Obviously the lounge, it was a large room with an expanse of plate-glass window immediately overlooking the front grounds towards a splendid view of the city itself.

Jamie was conscious of Logan murmuring something that she didn't quite catch, then a mature neatly-dressed woman came forward.

'Alice Campbell, my housekeeper,' he introduced, offering a warm smile. 'Alice, meet the soon-to-be Jamie Jordan.'

Jamie felt her face pale slightly, and she was conscious of uttering a polite greeting, although afterwards she had little recollection of what she'd said.

'I'll fix you a drink,' said Logan as the housekeeper retreated from the room, and Jamie managed a strangled response.

'Do you—lease all this?' she queried hesitantly, and glimpsed his wry amusement.

'I own it.'

'The apartment?'

'The entire building,' he mocked gently, and she uttered a barely audible,

'I see.'

'Do you, Jamie?'

She looked at him carefully as she accepted the glass from his hand. 'I didn't realise you were—well off,' she managed, taking a much-needed sip of vermouth.

'Does it matter?'

He was silently laughing, and she quickly veiled her eyes from the hurt she knew to be evident in their depths.

'Jamie,' Logan derided softly, plucking the glass from her hand and placing it down on a nearby table before pulling her into his arms. 'I'll show you to your room in a few minutes, then you can unpack. I have to attend a business meeting in the city for a few hours, but we'll go out to dinner and I'll show you some of the city's night spots. To-morrow I'll have Deborah accompany you on that shopping spree.' He kissed her briefly, then set her away.

'Deborah?' she queried.

'She's in charge of the office staff—very efficient, and possessing an excellent taste in clothes,' he told her. 'She'll take you under her wing for the day. Unfortunately I won't be able to meet you until later in the day.' He took hold of her hand and led across the room.

It was a very large apartment, Jamie decidedly dazedly long after Logan had taken his leave. Her unpacking completed, she soaked for ages in a bathroom the likes of which she had seen only on the pages of glossy magazines. Then, enfolded in a silk wrap, she had wandered through the many rooms before returning to her own to dress for dinner.

They drove out of the city, visiting a small exclusive restaurant Logan recommended, and Jamie sat very straight in her chair, eating very little of the many dishes put before her, and sipping excellent white wine. She was made startlingly aware of a different Logan from the man she thought she knew, for he had acquired a sophisticated veneer that both alarmed and frightened her. Even the car they had used tonight had been a different one—a sleek Mercedes sports sedan, the epitome of luxury. She felt as if she were floating through a dream, fearful that at any minute she might waken and discover it to be a living nightmare. She talked, smiled, even laughed, but all the while a tiny voice kept taunting—its tone derisive and faintly challenging. Why, when he could have any woman he wanted—why had he chosen her? An unpretentious, ordinary girl from a middle-class background. She couldn't even aspire to possessing wealthy relatives, or acclaim a pres-

tigious education. And socially, she was as far removed from him as chalk from cheese.

'You're very quiet,' Logan commented, his eyes
narrowing slightly. 'Would you like to go on somewhere where we can dance?'

Jamie forced herself to respond vivaciously. 'Oh,
could we? I'd like that.'

Certainly it was easier to go through the motions
of enjoying herself beneath bright lights with the
music wiping everything from her mind. It helped
when Logan held her close in his arms, for then she
could close her eyes and pretend nothing else mat-
tered.

They drifted from one night spot to another, visiting three in all, and it was at the last night-club they
came face to face with Sacha, who lit up sickeningly
at the sight of Logan.

'Darling! Where have you been?'

Jamie winced, and endeavoured a polite smile—
not that it was noticed, for Sacha ignored her completely. Logan appeared deliberately ruminative,
cordial, but only within the bounds of politeness as
he returned her greeting.

'You've met my fiancée, haven't you?'

Sacha's smile remained fixed, and although she
proffered a congratulatory spiel, her eyes glittered
with barely-concealed animosity. Then, unable to
resist the slight barb, she added, 'Not your usual
style, darling. I'm disappointed.'

'Really?' Logan drawled, and Sacha tried to cover
the indiscretion with a laugh.

'I don't see you as the marrying type.'

He threaded his fingers through Jamie's, then
lifted her hand to his lips, looking down at her with
such warmth her bones began to melt.

'I finally met the girl I want to spend the rest of
my life with,' he told her with sincere solemnity.

'Can you blame me for wanting to cast aside my bachelor existence?'

'Why—when you could be free to play the field?' Sacha arched suggestively, and he smiled.

'The "field" no longer holds any appeal. Now, if you'll excuse us?'

Wow! Jamie shook her head faintly as they moved away, and made a slight grimace as Logan gave her an enquiring look. 'You've hurt her feelings,' she declared.

'Oh, Jamie,' he derided gently, 'the Sachas of this world are remarkably thick-skinned. She'll survive,' he ended dryly.

It was well after midnight when they returned to the apartment in Kew, and in the lounge Logan regarded Jamie enigmatically as he shrugged off his jacket and loosened his tie.

Jamie stood there, uncertain and all too aware that they were alone, for even if Alice Campbell lived on the premises she would have long ago departed for bed.

'It's late,' she offered hesitantly. 'I'll see you in the morning. What time is breakfast?'

'Come here,' Logan commanded softly.

Her heart began to beat erratically, and she was conscious of the pulse at the base of her throat leaping with nervous tension.

'Not even a goodnight kiss?' he teased, and she swallowed painfully, longing for the security of being in his arms.

'I think I'd better go to bed,' she began cautiously, and he smiled.

'Afraid you might lose your head? I give my solemn word that I won't let that happen.'

She felt so confused it wasn't funny, and she could no more have moved towards him than she could have flown over the moon.

Then he was at her side, his arms crushing her against his hardening frame, and his mouth was almost punishing in its intensity as it met hers, ravaging with controlled passion until she was swept into a swirling vortex, incapable of denying him anything.

It was a long time before Logan loosened her arms from about his neck and held her away. His breathing was far from steady, and his eyes held tightly-leashed restraint.

'If it were possible, I'd make love to you now—afterwards you wouldn't be such a mixture of foolish uncertainty,' he declared emotively, giving her an ungentle shake. 'There's only one way to resolve this, one place—in bed. However, I've waited this long, I guess I can wait another four days.'

Jamie's eyes widened measurably, and she opened her mouth to speak, only to close it again as Logan pushed an angry hand through his hair, ruffling it into disorder, then he gave a despairing groan.

'Go to bed, Jamie. I'm going to take a cold shower.'

She hesitated fractionally, then turned and fled to her room, and the tears were welling behind her eyes as she closed the door, then crossed to sink down on to the bed.

CHAPTER ELEVEN

'ALL right, I give in,' Jamie grinned, spreading her hands in eloquent agreement, and Deborah nodded her approval.

'Mr Jordan will be delighted.' She consulted the list in her hand. 'Now, there's only shoes and hand-bag. When I return to the office I'll arrange for the floral bouquets, and make an appointment for the hairdressers on Monday.'

'You're very efficient,' Jamie teased lightly, and the other girl smiled.

'That's what I'm paid for. Now, shall we stop somewhere for coffee?'

'Please—my feet are killing me!'

'There's a place just round the corner,' Deborah told her, and Jamie matched her brisk pace.

It was a glorious day, the sun still hot despite being almost the end of summer, and this morning she felt much more her usual self. Some of her doubts had disappeared, and those that remained had been firmly cast aside. Logan had been particularly attentive over breakfast, apologetic that he couldn't forgo his meeting, but promising to make up for his absence by taking her out to dinner.

'I don't like to take up any more of your time,' Jamie began several minutes later. 'We've already bought the important items, and I've been grateful for your help. I can manage now if you'd like to get back to the office.'

Deborah looked faintly dubious. 'Mr Jordan insisted I was to stay with you until your shopping was completed.'

'Oh, Logan won't mind,' Jamie dismissed airily.
'You can say I was adamant, insisting on being independent,' she finished with an impish smile.
'Besides, I'd like to explore for an hour or two,
and I can't do that if you're with me, as I'd feel I
was merely wasting your time. In any case, he
won't need to know—he's at a meeting which will
take up most of the day.'

'Well, we are busy,' Deborah said cautiously.
'If you're really sure?'

'I'm not a child,' Jamie assured her kindly.
'When I'm ready to return to the apartment, I'll
simply hop into a taxi.'

An hour later she was carrying a few extra packages, and satisfied that her shopping was completed, she walked into the first coffee lounge she
happened to pass. It was lunch-time, and although
she wasn't very hungry she felt desperately in need
of another drink.

Walking up to the counter she selected a tray,
put a sandwich on to a plate, then moved to the
cashier and ordered coffee.

It was well patronised and there weren't many
seats left, but she found one and sat down, unload-
ing her shopping with relief. She took a bite of
food, then a few appreciative sips of hot aromatic
coffee, a slight frown creasing her forehead as she
reflected where she had seen a taxi-stand.

'Do you mind if I share your table?'

Jamie looked up, a polite phrase on her lips,
then she froze as her eyes encountered Sacha's
saccharine smile.

'Fancy seeing you here! Are you alone?'

Jamie's answer was monosyllabic, and the other
girl's expression tightened into disfavour.

'I'm surprised Logan let you out of his sight.
He's quite besotted, isn't he?' she trilled vindic-

tively. 'You certainly played your cards right, land-
ing such a wealthy man. He owns more companies
than he knows what to do with. Just think of all
that money, and how you can spend it! But then
you knew all that when you set out to snare him,
didn't you?'

'Strange,' Jamie declared sweetly, 'I don't feel
hungry any more. Excuse me.' She began gathering her packages together.

'Oh, darling, there's more,' Sacha informed her.
'Logan must hold the track record for infidelity.
There's been so many women—he goes through
them like suds in the wash.' Her mouth thinned
cruelly. 'Don't imagine for a minute his fascination
with you will last. Knowing him as I do, I'll be
generous and give you a week—maybe two.'

'By then we'll be married,' Jamie told her with
infinite calm, and Sacha laughed.

'These days, that doesn't mean a thing! A div-
orce is remarkably easy to obtain.'

'So it is,' Jamie said evenly. 'Goodbye, Miss Andreas.'

'Oh, call me Sacha, darling—everyone does.'

Jamie didn't bother to answer as she left the
table and headed out towards the entrance.

On the main street she hailed a passing taxi and
directed the driver to Logan's apartment, a cold resolve forming inside her brain. She needed time to
think, somewhere away from Logan's disturbing
influence.

When the taxi drew to a halt outside the down-
stairs entrance Jamie bade him wait, and as the
elevator sped swiftly up to the penthouse apartment she didn't dare pause and question her
motives

Packing a single suitcase took barely five minutes, and she hurriedly checked the telephone

directory as she made enquiries about the next
flight to Auckland, stressing that it was an emer-
gency and she must board a plane that day. Idly her
finger flipped the pages as she waited, then the
name she was seeking leapt from the page, the bold
typeface repeated three times, accentuating irrevo-
cably the business acumen of the man she agreed to
marry.

The disembodied voice on the other end of the
phone informed her that she had missed the direct
flight from Melbourne, but there was a connecting
flight to Sydney that left in an hour enabling her
arrival in Auckland mid-evening.

After that it was remarkably simple to address an
envelope and pen a short note to Logan, enclosing
her ring.

In the airport lounge there were several people
standing in groups awaiting their departure calls on
the public address system, businessmen jetting about
the continent attending board meetings, exerting
high-pressure salesmanship. Elderly matrons about
to embark on a visit to their family. No one looked as
if they were running away from anything.

At last the Sydney flight was called, and Jamie
followed the trickling stream of passengers out on to
the tarmac and into the huge jet.

It was late afternoon when they touched down at
Kingsford Smith airport, and Jamie lost no time arranging a collect call through to her parents telling
them the wedding was off, and she was on her way
home.

Auckland's International airport at Mangere was a
welcome sight, and once through Customs Jamie
emerged into the lounge intending to make her way
to the airport bus which would take her into the
city.

'Jamie!'

She turned, dropped her suitcase, and ran the few steps to where the two dearest people in the world stood anxiously waiting.

'Hey, little girl,' Adam Prentiss chided mildly at her sudden flood of tears. 'You'll drown me in a minute!'

Jamie withdrew shakily and took the handkerchief her father pushed into her hand. 'You came down to meet me,' she said unnecessarily. 'Oh, I'm so glad to see you!'

'Darling, you're so pale,' Mary Prentiss exclaimed with concern, then refrained from adding more as she felt the warning grip from her husband's hand.

'Let's get out to the car, shall we?' He bent down and picked up the suitcases, then strode towards the entrance, leaving Jamie to follow a few steps behind with her mother.

'Do you want to go straight home, Jamie?' Adam queried gently as they reached the car.

The thought of returning to the small town of Mangonui where she had grown up, where everything and everyone was so achingly, endearingly familiar acted like a soothing balm on her chaotic emotions.

'Yes,' she decided shakily. 'I'll share the driving, if you like.'

During the four hours it took to reach home, both Mary and Adam Prentiss sagely avoided any mention of Logan Jordan, directing the conversation on to innocuous topics and earning the undying gratitude of their daughter.

Mangonui was a small seaside resort situated on the very edge of Doubtless Bay as it swept steadily towards the northern tip of the North Island. With a natural love of fishing and boating, Adam Pren-

tiss had built his home within easy distance of the
beach, high enough to command a splendid view
out over the harbour. It wasn't a large house, nor
was it pretentious, but it was sturdily built and
comfortably furnished, and to Jamie it was simply
home.

Unpacking her suitcase in the rose sprig-papered
bedroom she experienced the feeling that she had
never been away. The years seemed to roll back,
bringing memories of schooldays, parties, sailing
with her father. They had been wonderfully care-
free, so obsessed had she been with living that no
young man had managed to even mildly stir her
emotions.

Because of the lateness of the hour, Jamie crept
off to bed after bidding her parents goodnight, to
lie awake until the early hours of the morning,
sleepless and tormented by Logan's forceful image. She groaned inwardly. Dear God, would she
ever be able to forget him? The feel of his lips
on hers, the way the blood sang in her veins at the
very thought of him? Haunting, provoking, *agonising*, until she could scarcely think straight.

The decision to take out the tiny seven-foot
dinghy came shortly after breakfast next morning,
and Jamie made a few sandwiches, filled a flask
with fruit juice, then informed her parents that she
intended going sailing for the remainder of the day.
Little could compare with the challenge of pitting
the small-sailed craft against the swelling tide and
the wind currents—to say nothing of the solitude
it afforded.

With the ease of familiarity Jamie rigged the
sails, then pushed the boat into the water, hopping
in as it skimmed out from the shallows.

The slight breeze tore at her hair and buffeted
the material of her blouse. Heading out from the

bay, she began to relax, for out here she felt free and at one with the sea, her mind uncluttered and at peace.

For five hours she tacked and gybed, relishing the fresh salty spray that whipped at her hair and dampened her hip-hugging brief white shorts. It was almost three o'clock when she turned the craft about and headed it in to shore.

The sandy foreshore was deserted, the only noise being the keening cry of the gulls as they wheeled out over the shallows, then almost floated down to waddle along the wet sand in search of food.

Jamie pulled in the tiny boat, took down the mainsail, and made the craft secure high up above the waterline. Then she collected her life-jacket and the flask and crunched her way towards the path that led up to the house.

'Mum, Dad—I'm home!' she called as she opened the back door, and was met by a rather flustered woman who looked far removed from her usually calm mother. 'Whatever is the matter?' she asked immediately, a small frown creasing her forehead. 'Dad's not ill, is he?'

Mary Prentiss shook her head emphatically. 'No, no, he's fine. I'm fine. It's just that we—that is, your father and I——'

'What your mother means,' Adam intervened blandly, 'is that we're going out to dinner—an arrangement that was made before you arrived home, and which we'd quite forgotten about until we were reminded of it this afternoon. It's one of those boring things organised to promote charity, and which we always attend with unfailing dutiful dedication each year.' He gave a wicked grin and placed an arm around his wife's shoulders. 'Your mother and I wouldn't even suggest you come— I've been telling her you're quite old enough to be left alone for a few hours.'

'I've left something in the kitchen for your dinner,' Mary rushed, glancing down at her stocking-feet. 'Oh dear,' she wailed, 'my shoes!'

'There's no need to rush, honey,' Adam consoled, bending down to brush his lips against his wife's temple. 'I'll get the car out, and by then I'm sure you'll be ready.'

Jamie glanced from one to the other, a faint puzzled frown creasing her expressive features. 'Isn't dinner usually around seven or eight? You're leaving very early, aren't you?'

'Mary promised to lend a hand,' Adam explained from the doorway. 'I'm a member of the committee,' he added by way of explanation before disappearing down the steps.

Jamie moved through to the front door of the house and met her mother in the hallway looking perplexed and slightly harassed.

'Now, darling, there's a dessert already made in the refrigerator, and there's cold meat and salad. You don't mind fixing it yourself, do you?'

'No, of course not,' Jamie declared with a faint smile. 'Dad's brought the car round to the front—off you go and enjoy yourselves.'

'You'd better go and change, dear—why not do it now, then you can watch television while you eat.'

'I'll get around to it soon. Now, off you go before Dad sounds the horn,' Jamie grinned, then she leant forward and kissed her mother briefly.

As soon as the car had disappeared from sight she closed the front door and made her way to her bedroom. Her hair felt dry and salty, likewise her skin. She would have a shower, get into something comfortable, then prepare something to eat.

It was almost six o'clock when she entered the lounge with her meal reposing on a tray. She felt refreshed and clean, her face scrubbed and shiny, and her newly-washed hair flowed loosely down her back. Deft use with a blow-drier had made it soft and silky, the ends curling slightly away from her face. The thought of getting into restricting clothes again hadn't appealed at all, and she had donned a nightgown and slipped on a silky wrap-around robe.

A thirty-minute comedy proved entertaining, and Jamie had just returned to the kitchen with her empty plate when the doorbell pealed. A knot of apprehension twisted inside her stomach, then resolved itself as she moved through the hallway towards the front door. This was Mangonui, where she'd lived for twenty years. There was no need for caution!

She opened the door with a welcoming smile, then felt the blood drain from her face as she stared at the tall solid frame silhouetted against the fading evening light.

Shock temporarily robbed her of speech and made her incapable of movement, then she attempted to slam the door shut, only for it to fly towards her as it was forced open.

Logan's face seemed more finely etched, and there was a network of lines crowfooting out from the corner of each eye—eyes that were darkly serious to the point of being almost unfathomable.

'Aren't you going to ask me in?' Logan drawled, and she began to shake uncontrollably, her voice a husky demand.

'How did you discover where I live?'

For a long time he just looked at her, then he offered brusquely, 'I had your parents' telephone number, remember? Mangonui is a very small town.' His eyes darkened fractionally as he slid his hands into his trouser pockets.

'What are you doing here?' she demanded.

'I could ask you the same question,' he declared with veiled cynicism, and she retorted swiftly,

'I wrote you a note.'

'Ah—yes. "I love you, but can't marry you". Just what was I supposed to glean from that?' He moved inside and closed the door noiselessly behind him.

Jamie worried her lower lip with her teeth, unconsciously biting through the delicate membrane until she tasted blood, and she was unaware of the flicker of pain that was momentarily visible in the dark blue eyes above her own.

'I though you were a road construction worker,' she explained tentatively. 'An ordinary man.' She faltered slightly, then went on with assurance, 'But you're not, are you? You're Logan Jordan—*the* Logan Jordan.'

'Does it matter?'

'Yes, *yes*—it matters!' Her eyes widened measurably, pain in their depths. 'I don't know anything about the sophisticated head of Jordan Construction, Jordan Consolidated, Jordan Enterprises —the list is endless, isn't it?'

Logan regarded her in silence for what seemed an age, then he offered slowly, 'I'm a man, Jamie. Fortunate, perhaps, in that I acquired vast holdings from my father's estate more than ten years ago. I wasn't born wealthy. I come from humble stock, and was taught very early in life that the combination of hard work and intelligent application brought its own rewards. By the time I went to university my father was a moderately rich man, and when I entered the family business five years later he had moved into the millionaire echelon,' he recounted quietly, holding her gaze.

Jamie lifted a hand and fingered her hair, a

gesture motivated by sheer nervous tension. 'Why did you deceive me? Wouldn't it have been better to be honest from the beginning?'

One eyebrow rose in cynical disbelief. 'The beginning, Jamie? You appeared like a mirage in the middle of that hot dry desert, and I no more wanted you at that camp than I wanted an attack of bubonic plague. Blake Curtis is an old family friend with whom I maintain regular contact,' he added. 'When I learned one of his foremen had been hospitalised, I offered to fill in for a few weeks. I was finding it difficult to end an—attachment, and it seemed like a good opportunity to get out of Melbourne for a while.' He paused, then gave a soundless laugh. 'At first I found it amusing that you should accept me at face value. It was a novel experience after years of being pursued for what my material wealth could provide. You could say I was world-weary and thoroughly cynical,' he commented with faint irony. 'When you returned to Alice Springs with your friends I had no intention of seeing you again, but after a few days I couldn't help myself, and I organised a trip down to Ayers Rock, sure you would accept—if only because it proved the opportunity to see that scenic miracle. By the time we parted at Alice Springs I knew I was lost.' He grimaced slightly, his eyes darkening with remembered anger. 'Do you have any idea how I reacted when I caught sight of you waitressing in that restaurant? I could have wrung your slender little neck!'

Jamie's eyes flew open wide at the quiet rage evident in his voice, and he uttered a humourless laugh, shaking his head in disbelief.

'Who could believe that a confirmed cynic like myself would settle for nothing less than marriage?' His expression became serious and faintly grim.

'Can you imagine how I felt when I arrived home last night and found you gone? Dear God, Jamie,' he muttered, 'that was the beginning of the worst moment of my life.'

Unable to refrain from asking, she queried tentatively, 'What about Sacha?'

Logan gave a low groan. 'I haven't lived like a monk. There have been several women, none of whom occupied more than a fleeting interest. You have to believe that.' He reached out and drew her towards him, giving a shuddering sigh when she didn't resist, and his mouth closed down over hers, gently plundering in a manner that sent the blood pulsing through her veins.

At last he lifted his head. 'Witch,' he accused vibrantly, his eyes dark with passion. 'Before we go any further, I have something in my pocket which I intend restoring to its rightful place.'

Seconds later the large diamond solitaire nestled firmly on her left finger, and she queried softly, 'Was Sacha the "difficult attachment"?'

'Yes—damn you!' His mouth swooped hungrily down on hers to begin a kiss that left her weak-willed and boneless, and he gave an audible groan as he lifted his head, then he began a lingering, tantalising exploration that had her clinging to him with shameless abandon.

'We're getting married as planned on Monday,' Logan told her, his eyes silently mocking her expression of disbelief. 'Tomorrow we leave early in the morning en route for Auckland to catch the afternoon flight to Melbourne. Incidentally, your parents are coming with us.'

'Oh,' she said, totally bemused, and was shaken gently.

'My darling Jamie,' he chided, 'you're showing a marked lack of interest——'

Jamie reached up and placed a hand over his lips, her eyes sparkling with humour as she shook her head. 'No, not true—it's just that you have a devastating effect on me.' She gave a yelp of surprise as strong white teeth nipped her palm.

'Be warned that I'll make a very demanding husband,' he teased, then his eyes darkened measurably as he continued seriously, 'I love you—more than I imagined it was possible to love anyone. You're my life, Jamie. Without you, I would cease to exist.' He bent his head and began kissing her with such incredible gentleness that Jamie felt her body melt from sheer sensual warmth.

'What are you wearing beneath this thing?' Logan murmured huskily, untying the sash about her waist so that the edges of the silky wrap fell apart.

A slow blush crept over her cheeks as he gazed at her thinly-clad body, aware that the silk nightgown clung revealingly to every curve.

'I think you'd better go and change,' he said a trifle unsteadily. 'If you don't, I may lose the tenuous hold I have over my self-control.'

Her eyes widened into large dark pools, and with a tortured oath he pulled her back into his arms, his mouth hard and almost brutal in its assault, then he buried his lips in the hollow at the base of her neck for endless minutes before raising his head.

'Go, Jamie,' he directed firmly. 'I have no intention of allowing your parents to return and find you in a state of *déshabille*.'

'You knew they were out?'

His smile softened his features. 'I rang your father just before leaving Melbourne this morning, and again when I arrived in Whangarei to let him know my expected time of arrival.'

Sudden comprehension lit her eyes. 'I see,' she said with a slight laugh. 'So that's why they both left the house in such a hurry! I wondered at the time—usually Dad is so well organised there's very little chance he forgets anything. If my parents haven't gone out to dinner, where are they?'

'Adam suggested it would be better if we saw each other alone,' Logan told her with a slight smile. 'He mentioned returning about nine, I seem to recall.'

At the smouldering expression in his eyes, Jamie stepped back a pace. 'I'll be back in five minutes. Go into the lounge and help yourself to a drink—there's an assortment in the cabinet.' She felt herself colouring as he gave an amused chuckle, then she turned and slipped down the hallway towards her bedroom.

Discarding the robe and nightgown, she hastily donned underwear and slipped into a dress. A few deft strokes with the brush restored her hair to order, and spurning any make-up she returned to the lounge.

Logan stood at the far end of the large room with a glass in his hand, and his eyes warmed at the sight of her, softening to such a degree that she began to tremble as an answering emotion swelled up inside her head.

Jamie said the first thing that entered her head. 'Have you had anything to eat? I never thought to ask.' She couldn't help the way words began tripping over each other. 'I don't even know how you got here!'

Logan began to laugh, softly at first, then openly so that his chest shook with it. 'Jamie, I hired a taxi from Auckland.'

She looked horrified. 'A taxi? But it's almost two hundred miles!'

He gave a careless shrug, his eyes faintly amused. 'If it were possible, I would have hired a plane.'

'And you haven't eaten?'

'No. Are you going to cook me a meal?' he began quizzically, and she nodded, beckoning him to follow her.

His arm reached out and caught hold of her hand, pulling her back against him, and her stomach curled alarmingly as he lifted the length of her hair and gently kissed her nape. 'I'm not hungry for food,' he said indistinctly, his hands caressing, heightening her awareness of him until she gave a muffled cry and turned to face him.

Reaching up, she let her fingers clasp together behind his neck. 'I love you so much, I *ache*,' she whispered softly. 'Are you sure you want me for a lifetime?'

His swift action proved more satisfactory than mere words, and Jamie let herself be carried away on the tide of his passion as he sought to obliterate every last vestige of doubt.

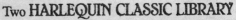

4 FREE
Harlequin Romances

Your FREE
gift includes

- *Anne Hampson* — Beyond the Sweet Waters
- *Anne Mather* — The Arrogant Duke
- *Violet Winspear* — Cap Flamingo
- *Nerina Hilliard* — Teachers Must Learn

FREE GIFT CERTIFICATE

and Subscription Reservation

Mail this coupon today!

In U.S.A.:
Harlequin Reader Service
MPO Box 707
Niagara Falls, NY 14302

In Canada:
Harlequin Reader Service
649 Ontario Street
Stratford, Ontario
N5A 6W4

Harlequin Reader Service:

Please send me my 4 Harlequin Romance novels
FREE. Also, reserve a subscription to the 6 NEW
Harlequin Romance novels published each month.
Each month I will receive 6 NEW Romance novels at
the low price of $1.25 each (Total — $7.50 a month).
There are no shipping and handling or any other
hidden charges. I may cancel this arrangement at any
time, but even if I do, these first 4 books are still mine
to keep.

NAME _____ (PLEASE PRINT)

ADDRESS _____

CITY _____ STATE/PROV. _____ ZIP/POSTAL CODE

Offer not valid to present subscribers

Offer expires March 31, 1981   R-2378

Prices subject to change without notice.